Books by Martha Bacon

Sophia Scrooby Preserved
The Third Road
In the Company of Clowns
Moth Manor

Moth Manor

Moth Manor

A Gothic Tale

by Martha Bacon

Illustrated by
Gail Burroughs

An Atlantic Monthly Press Book
Little, Brown and Company   Boston   Toronto

COPYRIGHT © 1978 BY MARTHA BACON BALLINGER
ALL RIGHTS RESERVED. NO PART OF THIS BOOK MAY BE REPRODUCED
IN ANY FORM OR BY ANY ELECTRONIC OR MECHANICAL MEANS IN-
CLUDING INFORMATION STORAGE AND RETRIEVAL SYSTEMS WITHOUT
PERMISSION IN WRITING FROM THE PUBLISHER, EXCEPT BY A
REVIEWER WHO MAY QUOTE BRIEF PASSAGES IN A REVIEW.
FIRST EDITION
T 09/78

Library of Congress Cataloging in Publication Data

Bacon, Martha Sherman, 1917–
  Moth Manor.

  "An Atlantic Monthly Press book."
  SUMMARY: A young girl takes charge of rescuing
a haunted dollhouse and the special dolls that inhabit
it from being sold to an antique dealer.
  [1. Dollhouses—Fiction.   2. Ghost stories]
I. Burroughs, Gail. II. Title.
PZ7.B1345Mo   [Fic]   78–59680
ISBN 0-316-07511-6

ATLANTIC–LITTLE, BROWN BOOKS
ARE PUBLISHED BY
LITTLE, BROWN AND COMPANY
IN ASSOCIATION WITH
THE ATLANTIC MONTHLY PRESS

Designed by D. Christine Benders

*Published simultaneously in Canada
by Little, Brown & Company (Canada) Limited*

PRINTED IN THE UNITED STATES OF AMERICA

To S.P.W.

in loving memory
triste loysir

Moth Manor

Chapter 1

ONCE UPON A CHRISTMAS morning about sixty-five years ago, two little girls named Sylvia and Mimi Wharton squealed with delight to discover under their shining tree a tall and spacious dolls' house.

"It's so beautiful I wish I could live in it myself," said Sylvia. "Why, it's like a palace."

"You could have adventures in it," said Mimi. "Strange adventures. Anything could happen in a house like this."

Sylvia and Mimi were pleasant girls with brown hair and pretty faces. Sylvia was at this time eleven years old and Mimi (short for Monica) was three years younger. They lived in a house called Wharton's Farm in the village of Westmoreland-by-the-Sea, which had once been a whaling town, and the dolls' house came from a second-hand shop on Main Street. The children's mother had fallen in love with it and repainted and refurnished it herself, turning it from a shabby old thing in a corner into a memorable Christmas present. Sylvia and Mimi were overjoyed with it, ignored all their other presents, and played with nothing else all through that Christmas day.

The house was indeed a superior residence. It had two stories with four high-ceilinged rooms on each level and an ornamental gable in the roof, hand-carved and painted white, with a round window opening into a storage space. The front door had a brass knocker in the shape of a lion's head, but the house could be disclosed to the world by throwing wide the partitions that formed the whole front. There were French doors in two of the upper rooms, which opened onto a balcony providing a place for those who lived there to take the air and to observe what was going on about them.

Mrs. Wharton had taken great pains over the furniture and decorations. She had collected a large number of diminutive household objects and had added several treasures saved from her own childhood to beautify the premises. These included a baby, finely made of wax with golden curls and real eyelashes, who lived in a cradle that was painted in the Venetian style with garlands and sphinxes; a Gloucestershire china spaniel; a canary in a standing golden cage, made in Japan, and a tea-set of filigree silver, complete with a graceful pot, a sugar bowl and cream pitcher, and six cups and saucers with spoons attached to the saucers.

The French doors and windows were made of real glass. A carpeted staircase led from the parlor to a small upstairs corridor. On the second floor was the nursery, where the baby lay rocking in its cradle, and three elegant bedrooms, the largest one draped in white flounces, fit for the Sleeping Beauty.

All the rooms were handsome, but the parlor was the most magnificent of all. A blue oriental rug covered the floor and blue silk curtains hung in front of the windows. A fire of red foil blazed on the hearth of a fireplace that was painted to look like marble. There were three pictures in gold frames on the wall, *The Infanta Margarita Teresa* by Velasquez, *The Blue Boy* by Gainsborough, and Sir Edwin Landseer's *Monarch of the Glen*. There was a bookcase full of books with gold-tooled backs. There was a blue sofa (with sofa cushions to match) and a variety of little chairs painted black and gold. Brass fire-irons leaned against the hearth and a grandfather clock stood at the foot of the stairs. The silver tea-set glittered on a japanned table in front of the fireplace. There were lamps and Chinese vases and a grand piano with a key in it. When it was wound up it played an old French nursery song, *Ah, vous dirai-je, Maman*, tinkling out the tune gently until it ran down. On one side of the parlor there was a library, containing a fireplace painted to resemble brick, more books, and the *Mona Lisa* by Leonardo da Vinci, framed in gold and smiling down on a desk that displayed a gilt inkstand, slightly outsize. A blue-jay's feather stuck in the inkstand made an admirable pen. On the other side of the parlor was the dining room, equipped with a long table, six Chippendale chairs, and a sideboard covered with flowered dishes. Beyond the dining room was the kitchen, containing every modern convenience and a dinner of roast chicken, a cheese with a bright red rind, a plate of apples, and two little decanters of crimson wine. These stood on the kitchen dresser between two copper candlesticks with candles in them.

The rooms upstairs were all furnished in the best of taste. The baby lay in its cradle beside the nursery fireplace with the spaniel and the canary for company. The house was otherwise unoccupied.

There were windows all around the house, and when Mimi pressed an eye to one of these she felt like a giant peering into a real house, seeing through the doorways into the rooms beyond. She half-wondered what went on in the corners that she couldn't quite see.

"Where do you suppose the people are?" said Mimi. Then she answered herself. "They must be in the garden."

"What garden?" asked Sylvia. "I don't see any garden."

"It's all around the house," said Mimi. "It's as plain as the nose on your face. You can't miss it."

"What's it like?" asked Sylvia.

"It's beautiful," said Mimi. "It has a fountain with doves around the rim." She was thinking of the alabaster bowl with four preening doves on the rim in her mother's vase closet. "And there's a big lawn with croquet things and peacocks and a little nut tree."

"What else is there?" asked Sylvia.

"Everything," said Mimi emphatically. "Everything you can think of. There's a stable like that one in the book about the Austrian horses, and a maze, like the one we saw in Williamsburg last year. And there's a little green orchard."

"Perhaps all the people are in the little green orchard," said Sylvia, "and if we call them they'll come."

"No, I don't think they will," said Mimi. "Because

they're not there. If they were I should have seen them. They must have gone to the desert."

"Well, where's that?"

"It's on the other side of the forest. It's an awful place. It's where all the lost things go."

"Is that where your galoshes went?" jeered Sylvia.

"Yes. And your arithmetic book — and the three butter knives that we had on the picnic last summer. Everything."

"We should go to the desert and look for the people if that's where they are," said Sylvia.

As it turned out there was no need to go to the desert. Sylvia and Mimi had several candidates who seemed suitable occupants for the dolls' house. Size was the chief requirement for tenancy. The larger playthings could not apply. But among the toys were two small wooden dolls in bonnets and crinolines, named Melinda and Belinda, a corn-husk dolly of unknown origin called Jerusha, and a soldier doll with a musket known as Colonel Charles. Colonel Charles had a black and white piebald horse on four wheels, simply referred to as "the horse," and Mimi said that he lived in the stables at the bottom of the garden and was therefore part of the household.

"They make a very nice family," said Sylvia.

"It was a good thing we didn't have to go all the way to the desert for them," said Mimi. "It's such a dreadful place." She could see the desert quite plainly in her mind's eye. Sometimes it surged in like the tide and caused the garden to disappear. It was a dusty waste like the town dump, encircled by low fires, smoldering against a white sky and cluttered with all the lost and broken things of people's lives. When it came creeping up, Mimi could always send it back where it belonged. She would simply close her eyes, draw a deep breath, and blow it away. But nevertheless it was always in the background, barren and menacing, lending danger and suspense to the already turbulent lives led by the inhabitants of the dolls' house.

They never lacked for excitement. They reveled in domestic strife and foreign intrigue. For one thing they were dolls with a past. With the exception of the Colonel, who was fairly new, they were of a considerable age. The baby was probably the eldest and was actually more an ornament than a toy. Sylvia, who was handy at sewing, lost no time in dressing him up as a king in a spangled robe and even made him a little crown so that she could hold a royal christening. Melinda and Belinda were period pieces, elderly ladies with sharp tongues, according to Mimi. They had come in a box from Philadelphia. Their hair was shiny and black, their cheeks were pink, and they looked as though they knew their own minds. Melinda, who wore a yellow crinoline, was the more benign of the two. Belinda, who was dressed in purple, wore a sly and malicious look as though she were plotting something. Jerusha was a complete mystery. She had been around the nursery as long as anyone could remember.

"She's been in the desert," said Mimi. "She was there for a long time. She turned into a mouse. Then Bael found her and brought her here." (Bael was the Whartons' cat.) "That's what things do when they go to the desert. They turn into other things — like mice and moths and spiders. That's why it's so hard to find them."

And it was true that Bael liked to play with Jerusha, carrying her around as though she really were some kind of queer mouse. She was made of a corn husk, but

Mrs. Wharton had refurbished her for the girls so totally that there was very little left of the original corn husk. She had repainted her face and dressed her in red calico, and she made a good housekeeper for the dolls' house.

The Colonel was the hero of the dolls' house, and Mimi and Sylvia credited him with a splendid, straight-forward character and a keen devotion to duty. He was a guardsman of the sort who are stationed outside of Buckingham Palace, with a red tunic and a bearskin helmet. He and the horse were inseparable. Mimi said that he was an orphan who had been brought up by his two aunts, the Philadelphia dolls.

Under the dispensation of Mimi and Sylvia, this household encountered almost daily adventures. They danced to the music box and cheated at croquet. Melinda and Belinda went sailing in a boat and were captured by pirates who held them for ransom, which Jerusha and the Colonel paid. Another time the two ladies made a trip to Washington, D.C., and horsewhipped a senator. Colonel Charles went all the way to San Francisco on horseback and captured an ivory elephant and an open-mouthed mandarin who sent up wreaths of incense from a wick inside of him. Jerusha went to a cannibal island and ate a cannibal. After the royal christening, which was followed by a feast of cake Sylvia had baked, the house was invaded by mice. The Colonel went to war with them, and after the mouse war (which ended with a treaty promising there would be no more cake crumbs) there was a revolution. A jumping jack was the revolutionary army. He broke his spring during the course of the revolution and had a funeral with full military honors.

"After all," said Sylvia, "he meant well. It was just that he was jealous of the baby. He wanted to be a king, too. It was only natural."

When they were not engaged in adventures or games, the dolls spent most of their time at tea or dinner, feasting sumptuously off the roast chicken, the cheese, the apples and drinking the wine. While the big dolls feasted, the baby would rock itself in its cradle in the nursery and think long, long thoughts. The baby never ate. He did not see the necessity.

"He lies there all day and thinks about the garden," said Mimi. "It's there when the moon comes up. All around the house. Then they all go out and play — while we're asleep. Sometimes when you wake up in the night you can hear them."

And it was true that in the night the nursery where Mimi slept sighed and stirred and rustled. The nursery was in the oldest part of Wharton's Farm, and one of its windows was half-covered by a huge honeysuckle vine that draped itself over one side of the house and thrust its fronds over the sill just above where the dolls' house stood. Moths and June-bugs and an occasional bumble-bee would get in and buzz about, and this was what caused the disturbances. Mrs. Wharton spoke of having the honeysuckle vine cut back but somehow it was never done. And Mimi swore that the noises came from the dolls, dancing in the garden.

"Or mice," said Mrs. Wharton. "Have you been eating cake again, Mimi?"

"The dolls' house is too grand for mice," said Mimi haughtily.

A few days after this conversation, the French doll arrived. She came as a birthday present to Sylvia. She was six inches tall, made of china and silk and sawdust, and she had golden hair and sparkling glass eyes. She came beautifully dressed in flounces and pink roses, wrapped in a swirl of silver paper. She immediately outshone the other dolls, who lay in attitudes of agony in their parlor while Sylvia adored the new arrival.

"There is no room for a French doll around here, giving herself airs," said Jerusha. "We have enough high and mighty dolls as it is." She threw a sidelong glance at Belinda as she spoke.

"I don't see anything so special about being French," said Belinda. "After all, we come from Philadelphia."

"You and your Philadelphia," snorted Jerusha. "What's so special about Philadelphia? New England is good enough for me."

"But not for Sylvia evidently," said Belinda spitefully.

"She is too blond for my taste," said Melinda. "And I never did care for that shade of pink. I much prefer yellow." She gave a dissatisfied twitch to her yellow skirts.

"It's affected to wear roses all the time," said Belinda. "And did you see her feet? Such smart black boots! And china from the soles of her feet to her knees. She'll be broken within a week. Mark my words."

"I wouldn't count on it," said Jerusha. "Something tells me she's going to be with us for a long time."

The other dolls smirked dispiritedly. In comparison with Sylvia's new doll they seemed crude and unlovable. Their flat features were painted on one side of their heads and their hair was nothing but a close-fitting cap of shiny black paint. Jerusha had staring shoe-button eyes, two round spots of pink for cheeks, a small triangle for a nose and a bright red smile. All three felt their disadvantages keenly when they looked at the newcomer. The Colonel and the baby on the other hand experienced no such emotions. As an antique of beauty and value the baby could afford to be generous, while the Colonel, though made of wood like the Philadelphia dolls, was not as pie-faced as they because his features were carved and he had been furnished with a nose. His uniform was smart and still fairly new and at certain angles he looked quite handsome. In fact, he immediately fell passionately in love with the French doll.

"It is my duty to love with a hopeless adoration this wonderful creature. I am dedicated to my duty. I never fail in it. I shall love her until I disintegrate, hopelessly, wordlessly, faithfully."

"Very touching," said Belinda.

"I shall serenade her from the garden as she sits on her balcony. I shall protect her against every danger that approaches. Little will she dream, as she sleeps upon her scented pillow, her golden hair spread about her, that I, mounted on my trusty horse, am guarding her from danger night after night."

"I suppose all men are fools and Colonel Charles is a man," said Belinda, much chagrined. "Nothing matters but being made of china and having glass eyes."

"It comes of having royal blood," remarked the baby. "Most of us have glass eyes. My great grandfather was king-consort of the kingdom of Broceliande in Brittany and I have my eyes from him. His son, my grandfather, married the Princess Aurora after he had awakened her from her hundred years' sleep. I daresay the French lady is some relation to me."

"There, you see!" said Jerusha, glad to see Belinda, that wooden snob, taken down a peg. "Philadelphia indeed."

"And in the meantime," sniffed Melinda, "what is to

become of us? Sylvia and Mimi think of nothing but that French chit. We shall be forgotten — lost. We shall wake up one morning in that desert of Mimi's while the Colonel is singing serenades. The thought is unbearable. It makes me hysterical." And she flung herself into a hysterical attitude, her arms and legs sticking out stiffly in four different directions.

Colonel Charles took no part in this discussion nor in any other. He was busy composing poetry to the French doll — odes, sonnets, and sometimes free verse.

"Poetry is a dreadful thing," fumed Belinda. "One can never tell what it may lead to. Now I suppose the Colonel will want to get married. Our only nephew!" She shook her head mournfully.

Chapter 2

THE FRENCH DOLL was called Henriette, but with
the passage of time she learned English and
altered her name to Henrietta. She was a doll of remark-
able accomplishments and perfect manners. She met
Jerusha's sulks and the sniffs and sneers of Melinda
and Belinda with a perpetual smile of sweet surprise, an
expression which became her and which she wore unfailingly. She seemed delighted with the dinner and with
the Colonel's serenades. The Philadelphia dolls continued to wear their bonnets and crinolines, but Henrietta was dressed in a style worthy of the Colonel's
hopeless adoration and received many new clothes from
Sylvia, who made costumes for her from every scrap

of finery that came her way. She was sometimes dressed as a shepherdess and sometimes as Cinderella going to the ball and sometimes in oriental costume with a turban and a feather. Once she even went into mourning when Sylvia got her hands on a remnant of black velvet from Mrs. Reels, who kept a sewing shop in the village.

"What a widow she'd make!" exclaimed Mrs. Reels. "A regular tragedian."

In all other respects Henrietta was a paragon. Her performance on the music box would have melted a stone. When she sat on the balcony in one of her grand dresses she made a perfect picture. She had glittering recollections of her former life in Paris, France, where she had been an ornament to society and had broken hearts at all the best parties. It was even rumored (by Mimi) that she had sung at the opera. "She could sing like an angel," said Mimi, "if only she'd stop smiling for a minute."

But for all her charms and accomplishments, Henrietta was no parlor butterfly. Like the baby, she was a genuine antique with no modern replacements, and she had survived wars and rebellions and had traveled by diplomatic pouch along with Important Papers to the little daughter of a French ambassador to the Duchy of Warsaw. Her courage was all the more admirable because, as Belinda had pointed out, she was so very breakable. She was unfailingly good-tempered and lived up to the house, her wardrobe, and the Colonel's courtship by looking her best at all times. In time, through her unceasing smile, she overcame the jealousy of the Philadelphia dolls and Jerusha and was accepted as an indispensable member of the household. With her good looks and interesting history she brought a glamour to the establishment in which everyone shared. Colonel Charles continued to woo her with soldierly fortitude and rescued her from deadly peril on several occasions.

There was the time when the nursery was repainted: the toys were moved temporarily to the attic and the dolls' house was besieged by a bat who had fallen in love with Henrietta. He hovered over her on leathern wings, his claws spread to seize her. "You shall live in my cave where I can look at you all night long," he squeaked, "and I shall never let you go."

Henrietta, smiling, drew herself to her full six inches and shook her gauzy skirts at him. "You will regret this impertinence," she cried. "Colonel Charles, be good enough to assist me in ridding myself of this bat."

Never deaf to a cry of distress, the Colonel came galloping up on the little horse. "Unhand that lady, Sir, or bite the dust."

The bat turned from Henrietta and made a furious swoop at the Colonel. Henrietta rushed from the dining room, where she had taken refuge, and threw the roast chicken at him, also the cheese, the apples and the two decanters. The bat in confusion flitted to the rafters, where he hung upside down, making faces at the couple. "What do I care for you?" he gibbered. "You're nothing but wood and china and sawdust. When *they* grow up you'll cease to exist. You'll just lie in a heap, staring at nothing. Nothing at all. The desert waits for you."

"There will be more children," replied Henrietta, smoothing her skirts. "Grown-ups and bats disappear. Children come and go and come again."

"You'll be a pile of musty rubbish in the attic," screamed the bat. "They'll throw you away and get new things."

"Drat that bat!" exclaimed Jerusha. "Why can't the

cat come and eat it? And everyone knows that the desert is nothing but talk. Nobody ever goes there. Not really." She shivered as she spoke. It was not pleasant to hear the desert spoken of lightly, or indeed at all.

"There's no need to worry the cat," remarked the baby. His voice rippled flutelike from the cradle. "Cats don't eat bats. He'll be driven out of the attic soon enough. Sylvia will chase him out into the sunlight with her father's tennis racket."

This was exactly what happened. Sylvia fetched the tennis racket, the bat sailed out into the noonday sun, gave up dolls, married, settled down in the barn, and was never seen again. Henrietta congratulated the Colonel on his heroism, but Belinda remarked that in her opinion the bat had never meant anything serious.

The following year Mimi became chief proprietor of the dolls' house. Sylvia was beginning to lose interest in it. She had been given a saddle horse; she moved into an upper grade at school. She was worrying because her hair was straight and the wrong color and she couldn't stand her nose. She was learning Latin, a language for which she had neither inclination nor taste and studying it took up much of her time.

"How time flies!" said Mrs. Reels. "Thank goodness you're still young enough to have some fun." She stroked Mimi's curly head. Mimi hung around Mrs. Reels's shop a good deal. Mrs. Reels petted her, scolded her, made dolls' clothes for her and seemed to enjoy Mimi's unwritten novel about the scandals and romances of the dolls' house. The house continued to be the scene of unbridled passion and cold conspiracy, and the garden flourished and expanded with every new adventure that Mimi could invent. Mimi never wearied of describing the fountains and the statues, the mysterious groves and secret lakes with which the property abounded.

"It's better than a tour through the Botanical Gardens," said Mrs. Reels.

"Grown-ups never see the garden," said Mimi. "They only see the desert."

"Go on," said Mrs. Reels. "Don't talk to me about that old desert. Tell me more about the garden."

"It's a wonderful place for a wedding," said Mimi. "Henrietta and Colonel Charles will get married there."

The idea struck her so forcibly that she immediately began to tease Mrs. Reels for scraps for a wedding costume. Mrs. Reels not only gave her the scraps but even undertook to make the wedding dress. It was made of white net over a shimmering satin petticoat, and the train was trimmed with swansdown and pearls. Mimi filched a finger-bowl doily from the linen drawer for a veil. Melinda and Belinda were bridesmaids in flowered organdy.

"Even they ought to be able to get a man with those clothes," said Mrs. Reels. "I haven't had so much fun since I was a kid myself."

"Isn't it wonderful," agreed Mimi. "I wish we could have a wedding every day." She helped herself to a cookie from a batch that Mrs. Reels had baked to serve as wedding cake.

"You can only have one wedding," said Mrs. Reels. "It spoils it if you keep doing it."

"I don't see why," said Mimi. "I mean to have lots when I grow up. They're such fun. We haven't anything for Jerusha to wear. She ought to have something."

"She's already sewn into her clothes so you'd better

just give her some flowers. I can't make clothes for her without taking her apart."

"Colonel Charles ought to have something special since he's the bridegroom."

"Bridegrooms don't matter," said Mrs. Reels. "Nobody looks at *them*."

Mimi did not think that this was fair. And as it happened, she knew of the very thing with which to decorate Colonel Charles for his wedding. It was a scarfpin, belonging to her mother, a little sword with a Roman pearl at the hilt and one at either end of the crosspiece. The crosspiece was set with three sparklers, red, white, and blue, and was adorned with scrollwork. Mrs. Wharton had bought it in Italy when she was a girl, and set great store by it.

When that afternoon Mimi asked to borrow the sword, her mother was hesitant. But since Mimi was now deprived of a playmate, because of Sylvia's having decided so suddenly to grow up, Mrs. Wharton was inclined to indulge her.

"But you mustn't lose it, Mimi," said her mother. "It's valuable. Those stones are real."

"I'll be very careful," said Mimi. "And it's only for a little while. Just for tomorrow so Colonel Charles can be married in it. It will be a wonderful wedding. We have cookies and lemonade, and everyone can come to it."

"Who's going to perform the ceremony?" asked Mrs. Wharton.

"The baby will have to do that. We haven't any clergyman, but the baby's a king and if you don't have a clergyman then you can use a king."

"I'm sure a king will do very well. You may have the pin tomorrow — just for the ceremony. Come and ask me for it when you're ready to have your wedding."

Mimi said thank you, but she was a little disappointed. She wanted to see how Colonel Charles would look with the sword before the wedding. She knew where her mother kept the sword. It was in the pincushion on her dressing table. So she waited for half an hour until Mrs. Wharton went into the garden to talk to Harry Hobson, the gardener, about the grape arbor, and then she tiptoed to Mrs. Wharton's room and borrowed the sword — just for a minute — just so she could pin it to a length of red ribbon that she tied over the Colonel's shoulder like an order.

Sylvia came into the nursery and stood looking down at Mimi disapprovingly. "Did Mother say you could have the sword now?" she asked.

"I only took it for a minute," said Mimi.

"You shouldn't have taken it at all. You should have waited until she gave it to you herself."

"She won't mind," said Mimi. "She won't even know."

"You'd better see she doesn't," said Sylvia. "And while you're about it, make sure you're very careful of Henrietta too. I don't want you taking her into the garden and losing her."

"Why should I lose her? And what do you care anyway? You don't play with her anymore."

"She's my doll and I don't want anything to happen to her. I shall keep her and give her to my daughters to play with when I grow up."

"Well, why shouldn't I play with her in the meantime?"

"Because you're careless and you lose things," said Sylvia. "You invented the desert just so you'd have a place to lose them."

"The desert was there before I ever thought about it," said Mimi.

"Well anyway, I don't want my things going there. I'm going to have lots of children when I grow up and I want my things for them."

"The way you act nobody will want to marry you so perhaps you won't have any children," said Mimi.

Sylvia walked deliberately across the room and slapped Mimi in the face. Then she stalked out of the room and went off to keep an appointment with her horse.

"You're jealous," shouted Mimi after her. "You're just jealous because you're too big to play anymore. And I hope *you* go to the desert and all your things too."

Somewhat relieved because she had spoken her mind, Mimi went on fitting Colonel Charles into his sash and had just stuck the sword into it at a jaunty angle when she heard someone calling her. It was little Sam Reels, Mrs. Reels's son, nephew to the gardener, Harry Hobson. He had come to play with her, a great compliment, or so he thought. He didn't usually play with girls, but the neighbor boys with whom he spent most of his time were away for the day and he was at loose ends. He bounced into the nursery, a plump little boy, a year or two younger than Mimi, with round gray eyes and hair that stuck up straight on his head, and said, "What are you doing?"

"I'm getting Colonel Charles ready for the wedding," said Mimi.

"What wedding? Weddings are silly."

"That's what you think," said Mimi. "This is going to be a wonderful wedding."

"What's that you're putting on him?"

"It's a sword," said Mimi.

"Let me see it."

"You can look but you mustn't touch it. It's valuable."

Sam squatted down on his heels beside Mimi and peered at the sword. "It's gold," he said.

"Of course it's gold. And that's a real diamond and a ruby and a sapphire."

"Did your mother say you could play with it?"

"Yes," said Mimi.

"Who's he going to marry?"

"He's going to marry Henrietta. The one in white."

Sam looked scornfully at Henrietta and then picked up Belinda.

"Who's this one?"

"That's Belinda."

"Who's she going to marry?"

"Nobody. There's only one soldier. She's a bridesmaid."

"She's funny looking. They're all funny looking. What a stupid game! Weddings are for stupid people. Only girls play at weddings. Ouch!"

"There's a pin in her dress and it pricked you. Serve you right. And if it's such a stupid game, why don't you go home?"

"It's bleeding," said Sam. "She's mean. She did that on purpose." He sucked his finger and eyed the dolls balefully. He didn't want to play at weddings but he didn't want to go home either. He tried a different tack. "I'll trade you for the sword," he said.

"Don't be silly. It's my mother's. And besides you don't have anything I want."

"I have lots of things. You don't even know what they are."

"Oh yes I do. You have junk. Your pockets are always full of stuff. I can't think what you want with it."

This was true. Sam was a famous magpie. He collected everything he could lay his hands on. The town dump was his favorite spot. Things clung to him and occasionally even seemed to attack him. He had been set upon by broken bottles and old rusty mousetraps more than once.

Now he leaned across Mimi and deliberately snatched the sword out of Colonel Charles's sash.

"You let that alone," squalled Mimi. "It doesn't belong to you."

"I only want to look at it," said Sam. "Why won't you let me look at it? And anyway it doesn't belong to you either. You said it belongs to your mother."

"Yes, and she'd kill me if I let you touch it."

"Why shouldn't I touch it?"

"Because you don't appreciate nice things," said Mimi loftily. Between Sylvia's slap and Sam's teasing she was thoroughly out of temper.

This last remark hurt Sam's feelings. "Who says I don't? I bet I appreciate them just as much as you do."

"No you don't. You couldn't. You're just a stupid boy. The sword is magic. It's got real jewels. Mother told me so."

"I like real jewels. Please let me hold it — just for a minute."

"You're holding it now," wailed Mimi. "Give it back to me."

"I think you're nasty."

"Well, if I'm so nasty why don't you go away and leave me alone?"

"If you won't let me hold the sword just for a minute I'll kill your silly doll. What's the use of a wedding anyway? I'll kill her." And he caught up Henrietta from where she was sitting in the parlor, all dressed as she was for her wedding, and thrust the sword pin into her. "There! She's dead. Now what will you do for a wedding?"

Mimi screamed. "You stop that right away. Give me back my doll. She's not dead."

"She's dead, she's dead, she's dead," laughed Sam, delighted to see Mimi apparently at his mercy. "And serve *you* right for being so selfish." And he danced around the room, holding Henrietta at arm's length with the sword twinkling among the bridal clothes.

"Stop it, stop it," bawled Mimi. "Give her back. I hate you."

"Mimi, Mimi!" It was Mrs. Wharton. The children could hear her coming up the stairs.

Mimi stopped screaming. She was terrified lest her mother come in and discover the scarfpin, borrowed before its time.

"What did I tell you?" she hissed. "Mother will be furious. She doesn't know that I borrowed the sword. She'll think we both stole it."

"Well it's all your fault," said Sam. "You took it. I didn't."

"Hide it. Hide the sword," whispered Mimi and she ran into the hall with the vague hope of preventing her mother from coming past the nursery door. Sam, now really scared, looked about him for a place to hide the sword before Mrs. Wharton should come in and accuse him of being a jewel thief. He was standing beside the dolls' house, and the small window, with the honeysuckle vine thrusting its fronds over the gable, caught his eye. Sam thrust Henrietta, scarfpin and all, into the vine, pulled at the fronds to cover her, and pulled down the window sash with a bang that shook the vine to its roots. Then he stood there trembling.

Mrs. Wharton swept into the room, greatly annoyed. "I could hear you two all the way from the orchard. Since you can't play nicely together, Sam Reels will have to go home. Now off with you at once. No, children, I'm not having any arguments. Home, Sam." And she bundled him out of the room, out of the house, and shooed him down the driveway. Mimi, shaking in her shoes, remained in the nursery and looked about for Henrietta. She searched the nursery and then searched it again. Then with despair in her heart she searched it for a third time, but there was no sign of Henrietta — or the scarfpin. She began to look in places where Henrietta could not possibly be and finally she simply sat, looking out the window at the honeysuckle vine and mourning because Henrietta was dead and it was her fault.

And while she looked, twilight came and a great greenish-white moth, with white spots like pom-poms on its wings fluttered among the leaves and drummed delicately against the windowpane.

"She's gone to the desert," thought Mimi dully. "We'll never find her. Even if we did, we wouldn't know her because by this time she'll have turned into something else. She'll be a ghost."

She went to the window to look more closely at the moth, as much because it was there as for any other reason. It was a huge moth with a wingspread of easily six inches. Mimi could even see what she took to be its eyes glittering in its face. It returned her look with a long look of its own before lifting its wings and melting away among the honeysuckle flowers, leaving a dark gap among the leaves. As it vanished, the music box in the parlor of the dolls' house gave a faint *ping* as though someone had touched it. But nobody had touched it. Mimi shivered. A rabbit ran over her grave. She glanced at the dolls, all waiting in the parlor in their wedding gear. They looked like corpses, lying there so still.

That night there was a terrible thunderstorm. Nobody at Wharton's Farm got any sleep, and the next day there was no wedding.

Chapter 3

WEDDING INDEED! It was a day of grief and a day of reckoning. Nobody believed Mimi when she explained that she had only borrowed the scarfpin from her mother's dressing table for one tiny minute. Nobody believed Sam Reels when he asserted with tears that he had put Henrietta in the honeysuckle vine for no other reason than that he was afraid he would be punished for snatching her from Mimi. And nobody could find Henrietta, although everybody looked for her. Harry Hobson even climbed up the house on a ladder and shook the vine. He shook and prodded in vain. There was no sign of Henrietta. The conclusion was that Sam in his panic must have actually thrown Henrietta out the window and she had been raked up with a pile of leaves and carted away. Anyway, Henrietta and the sword were lost, Sam and Mimi were in more or less permanent digrace, and there was nothing further to do about the matter.

Mrs. Wharton was furious about the loss of her pin. Sylvia was even more furious about the loss of Henrietta in spite of having outgrown her. Altogether, Mimi had a hard time of it. "Henrietta is in the desert," she told them mournfully.

"And you know who put her there," said Sylvia. "The dolls' house isn't the same place without her. And I'd counted on it for my daughters."

"I'm sick of your daughters," said Mimi.

For punishment, Sam was forbidden to play with Mimi, and Mimi was forbidden to play with the dolls' house. It was removed from the nursery to the attic until Mimi had learned the error of her ways and had repented of taking jewelry that didn't belong to her. Neither punishment really had the desired effect. Sam rarely wanted to play with Mimi in any case, and Mimi was so distressed about the frustration of her wedding plans that the dolls' house merely served to remind her of that blighted festival, so she was on the whole glad not to see it. The dolls made her feel guilty, lying about the dolls' house with stiff injured expressions, especially Colonel Charles, who struck her as more tinged with melancholy every day. "He should marry someone else," thought Mimi, "but I suppose he won't."

She blamed Sam Reels for being the cause of her disappointment, and sometimes she thought of ways to get even with him but there was no getting even with Sam. He was off with the other boys and Mimi scarcely ever saw him. When she did see him, he showed no sign of feeling guilty. He plodded through his days, sustaining cuts and bruises from all the things he collected, but it did not worry him. "I ought to throw the dolls' house at him," thought Mimi. "Then he'd be sorry."

As for the dolls, their days were darkened. The moon rose above their garden, but they no longer ventured forth to frolic around the fountain. No adventures came their way. "We might as well be in the desert with Henrietta," said Jerusha morosely. "It's got her. I know. That's how it got me."

"Henrietta is dead," said Belinda. "It's what comes of being made of china with glass eyes. That wicked boy stabbed her to the heart. I saw him do it. It is regrettable," she added, nodding to Colonel Charles, "but dwelling on the past is of no use. Even had you married Henrietta she would very likely have been broken sooner or later. You are probably well out of it. For my part, when I marry I intend to choose a partner of really tough material."

"Whom did you have in mind?" asked Jerusha.

"I've even considered marrying a person," replied Belinda, "a good, strong boy. Like Sam Reels. He's masterful but I think I could manage him."

"In all my experience," said Jerusha solemnly, "no respectable doll of my acquaintance has ever attached herself to a boy. There's no telling where such an idea might lead you. It sounds as though you were really hankering for the desert."

"Better than remaining in this attic generation in and generation out," said Belinda. "But perhaps I shall wait until Sam grows up to be a man. He might prefer it that way, and by that time I shall be a genuine antique."

"And what a good thing that is to be," remarked the baby. "However, I wouldn't be too certain that Henrietta is dead. The Henriettas of this world are not so easily defeated. I think we may not have seen the last of Henrietta. Dolls of her stamp do not die of pinpricks."

"Wherever she may be, I shall find her," declared Colonel Charles, smiting himself on the chest. "I shall seek her to the ends of the earth. Somehow I shall find my way to the desert and bring her back."

"Bravo," said the baby. "It took my grandfather a hundred years but he succeeded brilliantly in the end. No doubt you will, too. It's merely a question of time and looking for the right thing in the right place. Mimi has lost the bride and the jewel but some other child, some other time, some other where, will know how to find them."

"Child indeed," said Belinda with a toss of her head. "And where are you to find this precious child, may I ask? If I had my way, Mimi should be an old woman in the twinkling of an eye. That would teach her a lesson."

Melinda sighed in agreement and Jerusha wagged her head. "Children can be a great trial," she said.

"Without children," said the baby, "you wouldn't exist. Bear that in mind."

"What is that noise?" asked Jerusha suddenly.

"What noise?" said Belinda crossly. She disliked the notion that she might not exist. "Why must you always be hearing noises?"

"I'm not always hearing noises," said Jerusha. "I just hear one now."

The dolls fell silent. The summer moon cast a broad ray of light through the attic window that fell straight into the dolls' house. The beam touched the piano, which responded with a soft note: *ping*. Then stillness. Then another note. The piano was playing softly to itself.

Melinda gave a thin scream. In the moonbeam a pale shape seemed to fill the parlor window — a moth with huge greenish-white wings outspread. It beat faintly against the real glass — a thing of down and gossamer, casting a glow around itself through which it gazed with its two dark eyes, which sparkled like glass.

"It's a ghost," shrilled Belinda. "A ghost. The French doll come to haunt us."

"Henrietta!" exclaimed the Colonel. "We shall find her yet."

"Haunted," said Jerusha. "That's what we are, haunted. What is to become of us?"

"What are we to do?" lamented Belinda. "I am going to faint." And she fainted.

"Our guest and companion," said the baby softly. "There is no use in fainting, Belinda. We must simply get used to it. We shall see the ghost often. Again — and again — and again."

Very softly, the piano tinkled out the old French tune. *Ah, vous dirai-je, Maman.*

In her bed in the nursery, Mimi heard it. It broke upon her sleep and she sat up in bed, wide awake. The moon was at her window now and she could hear a slight throbbing at the screen as though the moon were trying to get in. She could also see a glimmering shape at the window, something fluttering at the screen, touching the wire netting as though it were a harp. She jumped from her bed and ran to the window. The moth was there and behind it she could see the garden stretching away toward the forest and the path that tunneled through it leading to the desert, where Henrietta lay lost. The path seemed to pull at her. She thought she might be sucked through the window. Mimi felt as though she were smothering. She tried to cry out but she couldn't utter a sound. She tried to lift her feet to run but she was moored fast to the floor. With a violent effort, Mimi turned from the window and the phantom that filled it and hurled herself into her cot, where she lay quaking in the darkness. She lay there shuddering for hours — or so she thought — hearing the rustling of skirts, footsteps on the stairs, a cough, a sigh, a door moving gently on its hinges. *They* were stirring about their house. She could see them with her mind's eye, huge as grown-ups, touching the piano, riffling through the pages of the books, twittering over the tea-set, plotting and contriving perhaps to descend from the attic and take her up to their house to play with her, to punish her for having lost Henrietta and her mother's scarfpin.

In the morning she told her mother and Sylvia that Wharton's Farm had been full of burglars all night long, but Mrs. Wharton assured her that she was imagining things. "Old houses always creak," said Mrs. Wharton, "and this is a very old house."

"There aren't any burglars around here but you, Mimi," said Sylvia. "You were the one who stole the sword." Sylvia was between the time for jewels and the time for dolls and she particularly regretted the loss of the sword because her mother had once told her that she could have the scarfpin for her sixteenth birthday. This anniversary was still some years ahead of her, but nonetheless she had begun to anticipate it eagerly.

"It wasn't me that lost it," said Mimi. "It was all Sam Reels's fault. And if it wasn't burglars, it was ghosts. And if it was ghosts, I think they should go and bother Sam because it was Sam that threw Henrietta away."

"There is no such thing as a ghost," said Mrs. Wharton. "Only very silly people believe in them."

Mimi didn't want to be classified with very silly people so she said no more, but privately the more she thought about it the more certain she felt that she had seen a ghost. She saw it several times that summer, fluttering around the porch light, its huge wings outspread like the skirts of Henrietta's wedding dress. "A luna moth!" exclaimed Mrs. Wharton. "What a beauty! It's the biggest one I ever saw." And watching the moth, Mimi heard, far and faint, the little French tune tinkling from the attic where the dolls' house was entombed, and the hair stood up on the back of her neck.

She fell upon Sam Reels one day in the grocery store and told him she had seen Henrietta's ghost.

"There ain't any ghosts," said Sam, but Mimi thought he looked a little green.

"Don't you believe it," said Mimi. "I saw it and I heard the ghost music. The dolls are mad at you. And if you don't watch out, they'll catch you and play with you."

Sam stumped out of the shop pretending that he didn't believe her, but Mimi thought he was properly scared. Sam told his mother about the ghost. She laughed, so he told his uncle, Harry Hobson. Harry was sleeping at Wharton's Farm at the time that Sam broke this news, because the family had gone to spend the month of August in New Hampshire, leaving Harry as caretaker. Harry agreed that there was something funny about Wharton's Farm. He was nervous sitting there in the kitchen night after night alone, and after Sam's story of the ghost and the ghost music, he became quite fidgety. One hot misty evening when a blurred moon hung over the pasture and distant thunder teased the sky, Harry was startled by what sounded like a tune. He heard it between two rolls of thunder while having a quiet glass of beer and reading *The Rose-grower's Manual*. He sprang to his feet, listening intently. Wharton's Farm gave a sigh and a creak. Then Harry distinctly heard footsteps, light ones, skittering across a floor above him. Harry rolled *The Rose-grower's Manual* into a weapon and went to the window to see what might be lurking outside. He could see nothing but the honeysuckle vine cascading past the window. The leaves rustled, although there was no wind. Harry turned from the window and again the music began. He could almost recognize the tune, or would have recognized it if it had continued, but it ceased the moment he concentrated on listening. It came from somewhere upstairs.

"I'll put a stop to that," said Harry. "I'm not going to sit here in the night and be haunted." Still clutching *The Rose-grower's Manual,* he started up the back stairs. The nearer he got to the attic the less anxious he was to confront the ghost, and as he approached the topmost stair, the stillness was so profound that it was deafening. He was on the point of returning to the kitchen when he heard again that faint *ping* coming from somewhere at the back of the attic. He stood still in front of the attic door breathing heavily and rattled the latch.

"Do you hear that?" whispered Belinda. "It's that gardener. He's seen her, too. He's angry and he's coming to seek revenge."

She addressed Colonel Charles, who was mounted on the horse, which paced restlessly up and down in front of the house.

"When the moon rises," said the Colonel, "Henrietta comes. That is all that matters. Let the gardener rage, so long as he does not harm Henrietta's ghost." As he spoke, the moonlight streamed in full at the attic window, drenching the house in silvery light. The piano gave forth a resounding *ping*.

"Stop that," shouted Harry from behind the door. "Stop that or I'll come in and make you stop."

"Now see what the ghost has got us!" exclaimed Jerusha to nobody in particular. "He is coming to destroy us."

"Do you think he'll burn the house down?" whined Melinda. "Oh, whatever shall we do? Would it help to have a fit of some kind?"

"Nonsense," interposed the baby. "He wouldn't dare. We have a ghost to see to it that nothing of the kind will happen. She will scare him to death and he will go away."

"But he isn't going away," wailed Melinda. "Why don't *you* scare him to death? Can't you make a noise like a thunderclap?"

"Unfortunately," said the baby, "I can't even say Mama."

"I hear you," bellowed Harry. "You didn't think I could but I can. Twittering and gibbering in there. Rattling bones and clanking chains. You think I'm afraid. I'll show you who's afraid." And he burst through the door into the flood of moonlight enshrouding the glowing shape of the luna moth. Poised over the gable of the dolls' house on a tendril of honeysuckle, it rose on enormous wings and flew at Harry, fanning his eyebrows. The dolls' house seemed to lean toward him threateningly. Something neighed and stamped near his feet. A dog barked. A bird chirped loudly somewhere, and over all Harry heard a cold trill of high-pitched laughter. He tripped over several small objects that seemed to have strewn themselves in his path and swatted ineffectually at the moth, which had fluttered well out of reach through a broken pane in the dormer window and now clung, shimmering ominously, to the honeysuckle vine. Harry caught up something — he could not see what it was — a small stiff object, threw it at the moth, breaking another pane in the dormer, and then ran down the stairs. The awe-inspiring laughter pursued him all the way to the kitchen.

At least that is the way the gardener described the scene the next day to his sister, Mrs. Reels.

"Nonsense, Harry," said Mrs. Reels. "You must have been drinking. Moths don't attack people. Bats, yes. Bees, yes. But never moths."

"This moth was big as a crow. It flew in my face and blinded me. Then the house rose up and hit me. I tell you, I turned and ran. I never stopped until I got back to the kitchen."

"Well, all I can say," said his sister, "is that I wouldn't put you in charge of a litter of kittens. They might scare you to death. I shall go and look in the attic for myself."

"And something laughed at me. One of them dolls was laughing."

"Or maybe it was the moth. I didn't know they had a sense of humor, but I guess you looked pretty funny, Harry."

"Garn," said Harry.

Mrs. Reels went to the attic that afternoon. She found Melinda in one corner of the attic and Belinda in the opposite corner. Jerusha lay at the head of the attic stairs and the baby was tumbled out of its cradle, crown and all, onto the crocheted mat. The spaniel was on the dining-room table, as though about to make away with the dinner spread out there. The canary, upside down, and the horse were in the parlor. Colonel Charles had somehow found his way into the honeysuckle vine, just outside the broken window, and hung over the gable entangled in fronds.

"Harry must have been drunker than usual," said Harry's sister to herself. "Imagine putting the soldier boy in the vine! Just like Sam said he did with the china doll. It seems to run in the family. I guess I'd better set this place straight, and then I'll lock it up so Harry won't be able to get in the next time he has the fantods."

So she returned the baby to the cradle, the spaniel to the mat, and set Melinda and Belinda in the parlor in front of the tea-things. She restored the canary to its place in the nursery and plunked Jerusha down in the kitchen.

"And horses don't belong in parlors," she said, putting the horse on the floor just outside the house and setting Colonel Charles astride it.

"You're the handsome one, you are," she said to the Colonel. "You hadn't ought to have attacked Harry. He isn't up to it. Next time pick on someone your own size."

And she locked the door to the attic and started down the stairs, laughing her head off. Halfway down the stairs she paused because she thought she heard something — a faint *ping* as though someone had touched the little piano in the dolls' house.

"It's the heat," said Mrs. Reels firmly. "Heat does funny things." And she went into the kitchen, closing the door behind her to make sure that she heard nothing more.

The story of Harry's misadventure was all over Westmoreland the next day and had penetrated to East, North, and South Moreland by the end of the week.

Harry Hobson had been savagely attacked by a moth and had cuts and bruises to show for it.

Most people laughed but Harry's nephew believed him. If you stick a pin into someone and throw her out a window, nine times out of ten she will come back to haunt you. It was a relief to Sam's mind that Henrietta seemed to haunt only Wharton's Farm, and he made a point of staying away from the old place. But when Mrs. Reels winked and taunted Harry with having run like a rabbit from a pack of dangerous dolls, Sam's eyes grew round as twenty-five-cent pieces, and he swallowed hard. The image of the doll with the jeweled sword shimmering in her finery bothered him. She had lain in his hand, her bright glass eyes staring at him. She had looked surprised but not dead. He did not like the notion.

When the Whartons returned from New Hampshire, Mrs. Reels did not hesitate to describe to Sylvia and Mimi how Harry had suffered under the assaults of the moth and the state in which she had found the dolls' house. And in the evenings when she sat fanning herself on her screened porch, while Harry drank his beer on the steps and the little frogs piped in the back garden, she would point to the moths circling the lamp on the table beside her.

"There's what knocked you downstairs," she would say. "Fierce, aren't they."

"It weren't one of them," said Harry. "It were a big one with white spots on its wings."

"A luna moth. There's one on the screen trying to get in. Watch out, Harry. What's the matter with you, Sam?" She turned to Sam, who was squirming on the hammock and scuffing the toes of his shoes on the floor.

"It's the moth," he said. "It's *looking* at me."

Chapter 4

THE PUNISHMENT, as punishments sometimes do, wore off after a while, and Mimi could have had the dolls' house out of the attic any time she had wanted it, but she didn't want it.

"What's the good of a dolls' house if I can't have a wedding in it?" said Mimi.

She kept trying to find Henrietta, poking fruitlessly at the honeysuckle vine and shaking leaves and twigs in at the nursery window but to no avail.

"Oh, who cares about a doll and an old scarfpin!" thought Mimi. But she went on searching anyway, thinking perhaps that Henrietta might reveal herself when winter came and the leaves fell. But there was no sign of her. The more Mimi hunted for Henrietta the more she regretted the spoiled wedding. Melinda and Belinda in their bridesmaids' dresses were a perpetual reminder of her disappointment, so one day she dressed them in their original clothes, stored the wedding scraps, the beads, and false flowers behind the gable, and closed the dolls' house up. She no longer wanted anything to do with it. Whenever she looked at it she thought not of the garden but of the desert.

The house gave her bad dreams. She would find herself standing alone in one of its huge rooms, wandering about in search of the lost bride, the lost jewels, aware of painted eyes staring at her through the darkness — silent presences thronging the stairs, watching her while she sought and found nothing. Then she would awaken to hear Wharton's Farm sighing in its sleep or to catch the luna moth drumming softly against the window screen. She wished Sylvia would hurry with the growing-up business, take the dolls' house away, and bestow it on those tiresome daughters. It bothered her to think of the dolls somehow managing on their own. Who could tell what they would be up to with nobody to guide their destinies? No good was what they would be up to, thought Mimi. She tried to shake this notion from her mind. She told herself that she was getting too old to think about the dolls' house.

For the years were gliding on. They glided very quickly. Now Mimi too had a saddle horse and had moved into an upper grade at school. As Sylvia had done, she was studying Latin and didn't like it. But unlike Sylvia, she found no fault with her nose nor with any of her features. She thought they were just about perfect. The older she grew the more satisfied she was with nearly everything about herself. She put the dolls' house out of her mind. For all she cared, it was in the desert with her Latin books, and she only remembered it when her mother complained of hearing mice in the attic.

"It's ghosts," said Mimi with a harsh little laugh. "The dolls are haunting the attic. Henrietta is up to mischief. Sylvia should take the house away. After all, it's hers."

From somewhere far away came the little tune *Ah, vous dirai-je, Maman*. Mrs. Wharton didn't seem to notice it, and Mimi put a ragtime record on the gramophone to drown it out.

Sylvia's eventual wedding successfully banished all thoughts of mice or ghosts or dolls' houses from everyone's mind. It went off without a hitch and nobody stuck a pin in Sylvia or threw her out a window. There were bridesmaids' and bachelors' parties and showers, and the wedding presents filled a whole room.

"It's a pity about that little sword," said Sylvia, tying a blue ribbon around her ankle. "It would be just the thing to wear for something old. It even had a sapphire in it — for something blue. Really, Mimi, it was too bad about that sword."

"If you don't hurry you'll be late to church," said Mimi. "It would be a shame to spoil this wedding."

When all the rice and rose petals had been swept away and the yards and yards of tulle had been put in a closet, Mimi had a last look for Henrietta and the sword, shook the honeysuckle vine, and even prodded the roots below the verandah, but nothing came to light. Henrietta and the jewels were gone for good. They were gone with Mimi's childhood and, thought Mimi ruefully, it would take a child to find them. She resolved to forget them completely. Their loss had plagued her for years and she hadn't time to be plagued. She had a wedding of her own to attend to besides, with more rice and rose petals and yards and yards of tulle. It was to be the first of several, and, looking back, Mimi always said it had been the most fun.

During the next few years Mrs. Wharton cleaned out the attic several times and planned on no less than five occasions to ship the dolls' house off to Sylvia. It never left Wharton's Farm because Sylvia had five little boys — Charles, Edward, William, James, and Henry.

Mimi, deprived of a wedding in early childhood, had formed such a taste for these occasions that it got the better of her. She had nearly as many husbands as Sylvia had sons. However, she had no children. There was nobody to play with the dolls' house, and it remained in the attic at Wharton's Farm and the dolls tasted death.

Mimi became a rather successful aunt. She was kind and generous to her nephews and they were all fond of her. They saw her at Christmas or on holiday trips abroad. Mimi lived most of her life abroad. Occasionally, as the boys grew older, Mimi would borrow one of them to take her to dinner or the theater. She was especially pleased to borrow the youngest one, a studious boy called Henry. She gave Sylvia good advice on the raising of children and took some credit to herself when the boys were successful.

The four older boys grew up to be doctors, lawyers, merchants, and VIPs, while Henry grew up to be a professor of history. He had two sons, but finally, to everyone's surprise, since the family had run so insistently to boys, he had a daughter. This happened just when Mimi had married a mysterious foreigner of noble birth named Mr. de Wardenour. Mimi, though shocked to find herself a great-aunt once again as well as a bride, agreed to be godmother to the baby girl and was flattered that the child was named for her: Monica Merri-weather Mills.

"No tricks now, Aunt Mimi," Henry had said when Monica was christened. "I don't want surprise packages. She's not to prick her finger on a spindle or spit diamonds and toads. Just let her have a good disposition and curly hair, if possible. I'm not asking much, mind you."

Monica was duly christened. Her disposition turned out to be admirable but her hair was straight. Mimi gave her a silver mug and went off to Europe with Mr. de Wardenour. For the next ten years Wharton's Farm was used only as a place for one or another of Sylvia's five sons to visit for a few weeks in the summer. Sylvia herself lived in California and wrote Mimi anxious letters about the place, but she was too busy to do anything about it. She complained in her letters that her daughters-in-law said that the house was full of moths and mice. Mimi wrote back that it had always been full of moths and mice and even sent a cablegram from Paris suggesting that someone call an exterminator. Nobody did.

But ten years after Monica's christening Mimi returned to Westmoreland. All the husbands, including Mr. de Wardenour, were gone, and it seemed that Warton's Farm belonged to Mimi since nobody else wanted it. Mimi came back to it in early spring with the intention of selling it, changed her mind, and decided to fix it up and live in it. It needed redecorating, and as Sylvia had said, the moths and the mice were a problem. Mimi summoned to her aid painters, carpenters, and the much-needed exterminator and then paid a visit to New York, where she went to auctions and bought furniture and curtains for the house. She hired a house-

keeper, a woman in middle life named Winifred Price, and a man called Fred Jackson to look after the garden and the horses. She bought a saddle horse called Nijjim for her own use and another called Sceptre and was kind enough to stable a third for a neighbor. This one was a mare named Taffy who was in foal. "It will be pleasant to have a foal about the place," thought Mimi. She also acquired a Pekingese, Ming, and a Persian kitten, Ban.

She moved into Wharton's Farm in the middle of June and spent her first morning in the house arranging china, glass, and linen and exploring the house from cellar to attic. She found her way to the attic quite late in the afternoon. It was a warm day, and Wharton's Farm had sunk into the quiet that Mimi remembered from earlier days as she climbed the staircase to the top story. She opened the door that led into the long, low room under the eaves where three generations of possessions were stored. The attic was dimly lit by its one dormer window, almost invisible, for the honey-suckle vine, which in the years since Mimi's childhood had been climbing up the side of the house in its leisurely way, had now reached the roof. The attic smelled pleasantly of mothballs and honeysuckle. Mimi paused on the threshold, blinking at the objects around her — several trunks, a rack containing a few garments — "they can go to the church sale," thought Mimi — a large chest that held hers and Sylvia's wedding dresses, a ukulele. Straight across from her, under the window, which had two broken panes, stood the dolls' house, with a few tendrils falling over its roof. It gave her a disagreeable start. It was silvery with dust and the recollections of things past. Mimi crossed the room and threw open the doors. The house was as she had left it fifty years ago, save for a spiderweb stretched across the parlor. The roast chicken, the cheese, the apples, and the two little decanters were on the dining-room table. Mimi put a finger to the piano in the parlor and it responded with a sharp *ping,* which made her jump. The honeysuckle vine stirred uneasily at the window and Mimi looked up in some alarm, but the window winked down from among the leaves, cool and glassy, peering at her. She put her hand through the little round opening in the gable and drew out the dolls, one by one, Melinda, Belinda, the baby, Jerusha, the Colonel, and the horse. They had been protected in their cupboard from the dust, and Mimi was angry to see them so unchanged. Such fresh complexions and bright eyes. It wasn't fair. Mimi was old but the dolls seemed to have discovered the secret of eternal youth. Mimi sat them in the dining-room chairs and stared at them. The dolls stared back with varying expressions. Belinda scowled and Melinda simpered. The Colonel wore his look of blank melancholy. "Still brooding over Henrietta," thought Mimi. And Jerusha looked at her owl-eyed as ever. The baby in his cradle gazed at nothing with expressive purple eyes, and the cradle rocked slightly, moved by something unseen. There was a draft coming from somewhere. Mimi looked up at the window and caught sight of a pale presence, greenish-white wings outspread and fluttering in the green gloom of the honeysuckle vine. It was a huge luna moth. It seemed to fill the entire window. It was looking at her, marking her every move. Mimi snatched up the dolls and bundled them all back behind the gable, overturning one of the dining-room chairs in her haste. She shut the house up and started to leave the attic, but as she closed the door behind her she heard the music box striking out the first bars of the old French tune, quickly, almost triumphantly. She almost ran down the stairs and into the arms of her housekeeper, who was looking all over for her.

"What's the matter?" said Winifred Price. "You look as though you'd seen a ghost."

"Nothing's the matter," said Mimi. "I saw a moth. It startled me."

Winifred shrugged. "Fellow name of Sam Reels called. He's an antique dealer. He wants to know if you have anything to sell him."

"Sam Reels," said Mimi. "I used to play with a Sam Reels. He was a funny little boy."

"He's a funny little man," said Winifred, "always pestering people to sell him things. Old gold and jewelry. He loves jewelry. Real jewelry."

"I haven't any jewelry," said Mimi, "at least not to sell to Sam Reels. He ought to know that. As a matter of fact, he was a horrid child. Always collecting things."

"He's still at it," said Winifred. "And they give him lots of trouble."

"Well, I daresay he deserves it."

That night Mimi was awakened by mice. They marched about the attic above her like soldiers and shifted furniture. They also skated, hammered nails, and did clog dances. Something twanged at the window screen. Mimi sat up in bed and could just see the shape of a large pale moth, glimmering in the moonlight and fluttering its wings against the screen. Mimi caught up a slipper from beside her bed and hurled it at the window. The moth disappeared and so did the moon, traveling westward across the sky, and the room darkened suddenly and dreadfully. Mimi fell asleep and dreamed a preposterous dream that she was old. When she awoke she found it was true. She *was* old. She got out of bed,

≈§ 49 §≈

went straight to the phone, and rang Sam Reels. She told him who she was — he already knew that — and ordered him to come at once and fetch the dolls' house away.

He was not very helpful. "I called you about jewelry," he said. "Old gold. What am I to do with a dolls' house?"

"Sell it," said Mimi. "Collectors love them. You should get lots of money for it. The only jewelry around here was lost years ago — by you."

"I was hoping you might have run across it when you was fixing the old place up," said Sam. "About this dolls' house now —"

Mimi interrupted with an alluring description of collectors from all over New York arriving to bid huge sums of money for the dolls' house.

"O.K.," he said. "I'll come and get it. My pickup's in the shop, but as soon as it's fixed, I'll come by."

When Sam had hung up, Mimi went up to the attic, half-expecting to see the dolls lying somewhere in wait to take her to task for having given them away. But a glance in at the gable seemed to show that they were all there where she had left them. She opened the dolls' house and glanced wistfully through the rooms as though she expected to find something — she was not sure what — and then she shut the house up again.

"Perhaps now you'll be quiet," she said.

As she came down the attic stairs, Winifred Price was standing in the hallway, looking up at her suspiciously. "What on earth are you doing in the attic again?" she asked.

"There was such a rumpus there last night that I went up to see if there was any damage," replied Mimi.

"You're imagining things," said Winifred. "It's your age."

"Nonsense," retorted Mimi. "You must have slept like the dead if you didn't hear it. It was mice, I expect."

"We don't have any more mice since the exterminators came," said Winifred. "And you're wanted on the phone. Long distance."

The caller was Mimi's nephew Henry. He wanted to send his daughter, Monica, to Wharton's Farm for a few weeks to be taken care of while he and Monica's mother went to London for a conference on the origins of the Thirty Years' War. He planned, if it was all right with dear Aunt Mimi, to send Monica up the very next day — airmail — from Washington, D.C. He would fetch her away again on his return, and Mimi would be richly rewarded for her hospitality by a visit from Monica's mother and himself.

"You'll like Monica," he said. "She's just your type. A wonderful girl."

"If she's so wonderful," said Mimi, "why don't you take her to London with you?"

"She's the wrong age," said Henry. "She can't sit around a hotel all day thinking about the Thirty Years' War. Besides, she's going through a phase. She's mad about horses."

"I thought the Thirty Years' War was over and done with," said Mimi.

"Not by a long shot," he said. "You've got horses at Wharton's Farm, haven't you? There always used to be horses there."

Mimi admitted to keeping horses.

"Perfect," said Henry. "Monica will be absolutely thrilled. I may have to let her come tonight."

"Tomorrow will be soon enough," said Mimi.

"She'll take the shuttle from Washington to New York tomorrow at noon," said Henry. "Then she can get the air taxi to Robin's Landing and you can pick her up there at three."

"That's thirty miles away," said Mimi.

"Leave Wharton's Farm at two. You'll be there in plenty of time."

"Who will meet her? I've planned to go to an auction."

"Send the new gardener — what's his name — Fred. With a horse box. She'll love that."

"How will I amuse a perfect stranger for a few weeks?" asked Mimi.

"She'll amuse you," said Henry. He clearly intended to have his way in this matter, and he was not Mimi's favorite nephew for nothing.

"In a minute or two," thought Mimi, "he will put up the phone and tell what's-her-name" — Mimi could never remember the name of Henry's wife — "and Monica that I've been waiting for this treat for ten years." Aloud she said, "Well, since you're my favorite nephew I suppose I'd better say yes."

"I knew you would. You couldn't have made a better decision. You're absolutely right to do it. You've solved the problem."

"Whose problem?" thought Mimi, as she hung up the phone. But on the whole she was glad that she had agreed to the visit. Perhaps a child was the very thing she wanted, a child with no past, only a future, and crazy about horses. She might have preferred a boy, but on the other hand a girl would be interesting for a change. And after all, this girl was her goddaughter.

She made a room ready for her great-niece. It was her room, the old nursery, which Mimi had redecorated and furnished with a once-again-fashionable mahogany bed covered with a patchwork quilt, a great bargain from one of the auctions she had attended. The walls were papered in stripes and rambling roses. The room contained a quaint and rickety desk, a large mahogany wardrobe, a Victorian washstand, and a number of china ornaments. Mimi was not certain how the room would strike a ten-year-old, but since it looked out on the pasture with the horses, Monica could always turn to the view if she got bored with the wallpaper.

Mimi inspected the whole house with her niece in mind. Monica would find it an interesting house, different probably from what she was accustomed to. Wharton's Farm was quite old in spots. It stood, so people said, on the site of the hen coop of the first Wharton settler, and there was a legend that some of the wood from the original hen coop was incorporated in the house. It was hard to imagine that this large, irregular white house with pale green blinds and the magnificent fall of honeysuckle had ever accommodated a hen. Its corridors, odd little passages, and unlooked-for cupboards would have been better suited to squirrels.

Mimi puttered around Wharton's Farm all that afternoon and well into the evening for the benefit of her niece, and behind their locked doors the dolls sighed and stirred, sensing change.

"Someone is coming," whispered Belinda. "I can hear things. And they are baking something. It smells like cake. Perhaps they have invited a child to stay."

"Child! What child?" asked Melinda. "Mimi hasn't any child."

"Well, perhaps it's somebody else's child, simpleton," said Belinda. "She may have a cousin — or a niece."

"Or a nephew," added the baby. "I believe she has innumerable nephews."

"A nephew would be of no consequence," said Belinda. "What we need is a niece. Mimi owes us a niece. It is the least she could do for us after fifty years of solid neglect, to say nothing of having lost Henrietta."

"It is a matter of indifference to me whether it is a niece or a nephew," said the Colonel, arousing himself from his perpetual reverie, "but a niece might be more likely to assist me in the search for my lost bride. Nephews tend to lack patience for that sort of thing. On the whole, I should welcome a niece."

"Fifty years ago I should have said that a niece was just what we needed," said Jerusha, "but since I haven't clapped eyes on one for over half a century, I have my doubts. Nieces may have changed along with everything else. I wouldn't put my money on a niece. Not until I'd seen it."

"Oh, dear me," fretted Melinda. "Are you saying that a new-fangled child wouldn't care for us? How distressing!"

"Calm yourself," said the baby. "Children don't change. They leave that to the grown-ups. I've existed — in wax — for upwards of two centuries, and experience has taught me that children are like us. They don't alter. They continue. The child, if it is a child that they're baking a cake for, will be what children always are. A year or fifty or a thousand — it makes no difference."

"What do you suppose this child will look like?" wondered Melinda.

"Like a child," said the baby. "In every particular. And a child will recognize us."

The piano, as if in agreement, gave a resounding *ping,* and the honeysuckle vine riffled its leaves at the window as the luna moth spread out its wings against the pane.

Chapter 5

MIMI DROVE OFF to the auction on the following afternoon accompanied by Ming. She had heard that there were a couple of Chinese vases that she thought she might like. They went for a quarter of a million dollars so she bought a butter dish with a silver-gilt cupid on it costing somewhat less and decided, before she was halfway home, to give it to Sam Reels as a reward for taking the dolls' house off her hands. She hurried down the highway because she knew that Monica would have arrived. Mimi considered that her niece was a lucky girl in being allowed to visit such a charming house as Wharton's Farm, and she had a short speech of welcome and congratulation on the tip of her tongue with which to greet Monica.

But when Mimi stepped into the hallway she saw no sign of her niece. She looked in the kitchen but there was nobody there. Winifred Price was off on her own affairs until dinner time and had left tea-things for two on a tray in the pantry.

Mimi went upstairs and poked her head around the door of the nursery. There was a suitcase on the bench at the foot of the bed but no other sign of occupancy. The bathroom down the hall was as she had left it that morning, the guest towels untouched on the racks. Perhaps Monica was at the stables getting acquainted with the horses, but when Mimi looked out of the bedroom window she could see the three grazing placidly and alone at the far end of the meadow under the apple trees.

Puzzled, Mimi stepped out into the corridor. The corrider was long, narrow, and windowless. At one end of it a steep flight of red-carpeted stairs led to the attic. Seated on the topmost stair and peeping through the banister rails was a girl of about ten with gray eyes and two brown braids falling over her shoulders, comfortably dressed in blue jeans and a red shirt.

Mimi stopped short and gave a little cough. The girl's eyebrows shot up but she said nothing. She seemed to think that Mimi should speak first. The two stared at each other. Finally Mimi spoke.

"What on earth are you doing? I thought you'd be out with the horses."

"The man said I wasn't to ride until my aunt came. Are you my aunt?"

"Yes. That is, if you're Monica Mills, I am."

"I'm Monica Mills, all right."

"What are you doing up in the attic?"

"I was exploring."

"Oh, I see. Well, there's really nothing to explore.

You'd better come on down. It's time for tea. I hope you had a good flight."

"It was uneventful," said Monica. She rose to her feet and started slowly, almost reluctantly, down the stairs. "Nothing happened. We didn't crash or anything." She paused and looked over her shoulder. "There's lots to explore," she said gently. "There's a doll's house up there."

"Oh," said Mimi vaguely. "That old thing."

"It's beautiful," said Monica. "It looks as though someone still lived there."

"Nobody lives there," said Mimi irritably.

"There's a meal on the table," persisted Monica. "Someone interrupted it. Everyone pushed their chairs back suddenly and left the table."

"Do come and have tea," said Mimi. "You must be starved."

"I ate on the plane," said Monica. However, she came the rest of the way down the stairs and followed her aunt obediently into the parlor. Mimi supplied the child with tea and a slice of cake, helped herself to a cup, and the two sat and eyed each other across the tea-things.

"You may ride Nijjim when you've finished if you'd care to," said Mimi presently.

"Thank you. I'd like to very much." She took a large bite of cake. "Did the dolls' house belong to you?"

"Yes," said Mimi, "to me and my sister."

"That's my grandmother," said Monica, "so I suppose it belongs partly to me too."

"Unfortunately," replied Mimi, "it doesn't belong to any of us anymore because I've just agreed to give it away."

"Give it away!"

"Yes." Mimi's voice came out high and childish, an echo of Monica's. "Why not? It never occurred to me that anyone would want it. I've given it to the antique dealer." Mimi thrust a cigarette into a long holder, lit it, and turned her bluish curly-haired head toward the window in order to avoid Monica's level gray eyes. "He's coming to fetch it in a day or two."

"What would the antique dealer want with it? Can he play with it?"

"No, of course not. He's an old —" Mimi paused remembering that Sam Reels was younger than she was. "Well he isn't all that old. I mean to say he's a man and the house is an antique and he sells them."

Monica sighed. "I wish he'd sell it to me. But I don't suppose I could afford it."

"Perhaps you could take a mortgage on it," said Mimi jokingly.

But Monica did not seem to be in the mood for jokes. Her expression was disappointed and melancholy. "Tell me about the house," she said. "Tell me about when you were a little girl. What was it like in the old-fashioned days? Did you wear a hoopskirt and lace trousers when you played with it?"

"I didn't play with it all that much," said Mimi with some heat. "And I certainly didn't wear a hoopskirt. I'm a product of this century. I was a flapper." Mimi drew on her cigarette and looped the string of pearls, which she habitually wore dangling nearly to her waist, around her fingers.

"I thought you said the house was an antique," said Monica.

"It is. But I'm not. How old do you think I am anyway?"

Monica looked at her intently. "About fifty-five —
or eighty. No, you're younger than eighty. Anyone can
see that."

"Thank you," said Mimi coldly.

"You're welcome," returned Monica, ignoring the
chill in her aunt's voice. "Tell me about the people in
the house."

"People? What people?"

"The dolls. I found them in a hole at the top of the
house."

"Oh, those. They're just little dolls. Silly little dolls.
I put them up in the gable. You should have left them
alone. It's naughty to meddle with things that don't
belong to you."

"All I did was put them back in the dining room,"
said Monica. "Why did you stuff them into that poky
little place?"

"Because they were noisy," said Mimi, not thinking
what she was saying.

"Noisy? What kind of noise do they make?"

"Oh, really," said Mimi, "it's the attic. This is an old
house. It settles. I put them up behind the gable because
I was clearing out the attic. Why don't you go and see
about the horses? Fred will tack up Nijjim for you. It's
two hours until dinner. You can ride around the orchard
or you could take the little circle up through the woods.
Nijjim knows it. You've plenty of time. It won't be dark
for ages."

Monica put down her teacup and carefully licked her
fingers free of cake crumbs. "I don't mind the dark. I'd
like to ride in the dark. And I want to hear more about
the house."

"I've told you all that I remember," said Mimi.

"There's a horse in the dolls' house," said Monica. "A little black and white silky horse. He looks like your Nijjim. What sort of name is Nijjim?"

"It's Arabic for Star."

"That's a nice name for a horse. He's got four wheels and a very nice bridle with rosettes on it. Someone left him upside down in the library. That's a pretty funny place to leave a horse."

"It was unpardonably careless of someone," said Mimi sarcastically. "The least they could have done was to put him in the stables."

"Oh, are there stables somewhere?"

"I imagine we used to pretend that there were stables. We used to say that there was a garden — a beautiful garden."

"Oh," sighed Monica, "what was it like?"

"It was all nonsense," said Mimi, rousing herself. "I couldn't begin to tell you about it because I've forgotten."

"Did the dolls have names?" asked Monica.

"What a little bulldog you are!" exclaimed Mimi. "Yes, they had names. Dolls always have names. Silly names. Sylvia named them. She liked naming things. There was Melinda and Belinda — they were old-fashioned wooden dolls — and Jerusha, and a soldier doll called Colonel Charles, and there was King Edward. He was a wax baby. And then there was the doll who became a ghost."

"A ghost!"

"Her name was Henrietta. She was a china doll with golden hair. And one day —" Mimi stopped and shut her mouth with a snap. She didn't want to go into the details of Henrietta's disappearance.

"She simply vanished into thin air with my mother's scarfpin," concluded Mimi. "So she must have become a ghost. Only ghosts can melt away like that."

"What was she doing with your mother's scarfpin?"

"She was all dressed up for a wedding. We were going to marry her to Colonel Charles. He was supposed to wear the pin because it looked like a sword, but it was stuck in Henrietta's clothes, and then she and the pin disappeared. She was simply gone."

"And you never saw her again after that? And you never had the wedding?"

"No. That was the end of it."

"How dreadful."

"It was very disappointing," said Mimi.

"Yes," said Monica. "How sad for Colonel Charles! No wonder he has that gloomy look. It must be awful to be deprived of a wedding like that."

"Awful," agreed Mimi.

"Didn't you ever look for the bride?" asked Monica.

"Oh, I looked for her. And Sylvia hunted high and low and accused me of stealing. But Henrietta was not to be found. Anyway, it's all over now. The house is off my hands, and if it leads Sam Reels a dance more's the pity. It's been cluttering up the attic far too long. I should have packed it off years ago."

"I wish I might have kept the house," sighed Monica, almost to herself. "And it's such a shame about the wedding."

"It was all nonsense," said Mimi. "And the house was a nuisance. I was always in trouble over that house. It's a relief to know that it's going. The desert will get it in the end, I expect."

"The desert?"

"It's where things get lost. All the old useless things."

"But the house isn't old and useless. And neither are the dolls. They're young. They stay that way."

"Nothing stays that way. That's why everything goes to the desert."

"I bet the bride is in the desert and if we only knew how to get there we could find her and bring her back and we could have the wedding after all — in the garden."

"I expect the garden's in the desert too," said Mimi and gave herself a shake. "And that reminds me. I ought to give a garden party so you can meet some people. You mustn't be allowed to spend the summer mooning over old toys in attics. You should get to know some young people. I should invite a lot of people with children your age, so that you can have healthy outdoor amusements and make lasting friendships."

"I can ride Nijjim," said Monica. "And I have lasting friendships at home."

She was not particularly anxious to meet a lot of children her age. There was a great deal to think about at Wharton's Farm, and Monica had discovered some time before her tenth birthday that children her own age did not necessarily sympathize with her views of things. It had always mystified her that older people were so ready to assume that another child "just your age" was bound to be a desirable companion. What would her aunt think now, Monica wondered, if she were to produce a grown-up, just Aunt Mimi's age, whatever that might be, and insist that they love each other?

"You need a varied social life," continued Aunt Mimi. "Everybody does. I shall give this party especially for you."

"Thank you," said Monica without enthusiasm.

"You're welcome." Mimi glanced suspiciously at her niece. She distrusted a girl who would not jump at a party. "Why don't you go and ride? There are real horses out there. It's time you did something about them."

This time Monica went. Mimi was relieved to see her a few minutes later, standing in the meadow, her head close to Nijjim's, evidently talking to him. Nijjim was listening attentively. Once or twice he pawed the ground with his foot. Once he neighed softly. The sound came to Mimi's ears on the breeze.

"What can they be talking about?" she wondered.

Presently Monica led the horse to the stable and a short while later brought him out, saddled and bridled. She mounted him and rode off toward the woods.

"Good," thought Mimi. "At least her mind's off the dolls' house. Nijjim will keep her busy."

Chapter 6

MONICA TOOK PAINS over her appearance that evening. She changed her jeans for a long dress, a blue one with white dots and the only dress she'd brought. She thought her aunt might be interested in clothes. Indeed, Mimi loved clothes, and the two talked animatedly about fashions, past and present, throughout dinner. They dined on a small screened porch off the dining room, overlooking the meadow. As the twilight deepened the little tree-toads piped up, and presently the meadow brightened under the light of a full moon. Monica was pleased to be eating dinner by moonlight and dawdled comfortably over a second dish of ice cream. The moon rose steadily, pouring forth a stream of pale fire. The porch screen hummed, it seemed, to the sound of the moon.

"Oh, look, a butterfly!" Monica pointed with her spoon to an upper corner of the screen where a large luna moth with luminous white spots on its wings was beating against the wire.

Mimi caught her breath. "Really!" she exclaimed. "I shall have to call the exterminators if we are to be harried night and day by that insect. And it's not a butterfly. It's a luna moth."

"Did it come from the moon?" asked Monica fancifully.

"No," said Mimi. "It came from a caterpillar. It's just an ordinary bug."

"Well, I don't call it ordinary," said Monica. "It looks very *extra*ordinary to me. It looks like a lady in a big skirt. Perhaps it's someone who got changed into a moth."

From where he was sitting at the other end of the porch, Ban, the kitten, rose on tiptoes, arched his back, and spat softly.

Mimi also made a slight hissing sound as she drew in her breath sharply. "What a queer idea! It's nothing of the kind. Moths always come to a light. There's nothing extraordinary about it at all. And I think it's time you went to bed. You must be tired after flying around all day."

"I only flew for a couple of hours," said Monica.

"Flying is very exhausting," said Mimi. "Run along to bed."

Monica went. She ascended the stairs to the sound of strangled sobs and gunshots — Winifred Price was watching a television show — and thought with regret that she had gained an aunt but lost a dolls' house.

She would willingly have lost the aunt instead. Not that she had taken a dislike to her aunt, exactly. In some ways she quite liked her. Monica's father had boasted that his aunt was an international beauty, and though Mimi was not precisely beautiful in her niece's eyes, Monica thought her glamorous with her feathery blue hair, her long, lean figure, and her rope of pearls, the whole effect made mysterious by a cloud of cigarette smoke.

But like all mysteries, Mimi was a little scary. She obviously did not appreciate the wonderful dolls' house. It had not escaped Monica that Mimi seemed actually to dislike it, calling it "that old thing." And she had given it away to the antique dealer. He would come to fetch it, Monica supposed, before she had had a chance to halfway investigate its treasures. Even the short while she had spent with it that afternoon before her aunt's return had convinced her that it was a house of marvels. She pondered them as she made ready for sleep. Her mind dwelt upon a tea-set of silver filigree, complete in every part, even to the spoons attached to the saucers. It was fit for an empress, for Princess Aurora or fair Snow White. Nor could she forget the cradle with its sphinxes and wreaths, nor the spaniel, so elegant and appealing on his mat. What fine wines ripened in those decanters! And what strange tales lay unread in the pages of those books! Monica could almost have wept that all this must fall into the hands of an unfeeling antique dealer.

Her aunt had mentioned a garden. Monica had no difficulty in imagining it, its sweep of lawn, peacocks spreading their fans in the sunlight, flowering trees, a fountain with doves cooing at the rim, marble statues glimmering in groves of cypress and yew, from which one step led to the forest without an end.

Monica climbed into the mahogany bed and was followed by the kitten, who took possession of most of it, as cats will when they share sleeping quarters. Monica managed to dispose herself around him, only to be disturbed by a telephone call from her parents, whom she had promised to ring up on arrival. After putting them out of their misery by assuring them that she had not fallen out of the plane, she returned to bed and fell asleep with a bang.

She slept for several hours — or so she thought — perhaps it was only for a few minutes — but she was suddenly wide awake. The moon had awakened her, she supposed. It was shining full-faced through the window that looked out across the meadow, casting its beam athwart the patchwork quilt, edging the drowsing cat in silver. It was so bright that she could not only see it but hear it because it drummed faintly against the window screen.

Monica sat up in bed and stared at the moon. The drumming continued. She crawled to the foot of the bed and saw plainly the luna moth with its great wings spread out against the screen. It wanted to come in.

Monica ran to the window, found the catch on the screen, and lifted it, allowing the moth to slip into the room. Once inside, it circled the room slowly and then flew toward the door, which was slightly ajar, and out into the hallway. Monica, barefoot and wearing only a summer nightgown, followed it into the corridor.

She noticed that the corridor was chilly in spite of the balminess of the summer night. The moth hovered over her just out of reach, but it showed no sign of trying to escape from her, and Monica pursued it, trying to find out where it wanted to go. The corridor was dark, much darker than the bedroom, but the moth was clearly visible, as though it carried its own glow with it. It flew up to the molding above the attic stairs, paused, seemed to take its bearings, and then drifted up the stairwell. Keeping the moth in view, Monica crept up the stairs and reached the top, scarcely knowing how she had got there. Suddenly the moth vanished. There was only darkness where it had been floating above her head a second before. Then something touched her hand. She looked down and saw that the moth was perched on the latch of the door to the attic before which she was standing. She put out her hand to lift the latch and was checked by a sound. It was such a small sound and it ceased so abruptly that Monica doubted the second after it occurred that she had heard it at all. She stood stock-still listening. The house was quiet as a grave. The moth, poised on the latch, lifted its wings. Again Monica put her hand out. The sound repeated itself, two tinkling notes: *ping — ping.*

Ping — ping. It sounded like a music box, thought Monica. It also sounded very far away. Or was it so far away, she wondered, as long ago? Two thin notes, the beginning of a tune, chimed at the edge of her memory. She held her breath, trying to hear them again, as though she could induce them to sound by concentrating. But they were not repeated. Instead she heard a rustling, sighing sound, as though something were blowing across the floor of the attic — something small on tiny feet.

"Mice?" thought Monica.

Something brushed her ankles as delicately as feathers. Ban's tail. He had followed her on his mossy feet and was crouched at the attic door, his nose to the crack, at the threshold. Monica opened the door and found herself standing in a shower of moonlight. The moth flew into the beam and hung there, its wings almost spanning it. Then, while she watched, it flew toward the

window, where the white gable of the dolls' house stood out against the darkness. The luminous wings shaped themselves over the gable for an instant, and then the moth vanished again.

Ping-ping-ping-ping. The sound came from the dolls' house. The piano in the parlor was playing its tune. Ban, caught in the moonbeam, fluffed out his tail.

Monica crept across the attic and peeped through one of the front windows into the dolls' house. The moonlight revealed the house in all its quiet perfection. It seemed to breathe as though it were alive and dreaming. A breeze plucked at the parlor curtains and even gently lifted the hair on Monica's forehead.

"How large this house is," thought Monica. "It almost seems to have grown since this afternoon. Whoever heard of a house growing! But it's either that or I've shrunk." She had dropped to her knees to peer through the parlor window, but now the house seemed to fill her whole field of vision, and she thought it was silly to be crouching in front of it like a small animal. So she rose to her feet and opened the front door. She found herself in the parlor, which was empty, but she could hear voices coming from the dining room. Several people seemed to be engaged in lively conversation.

"It almost sounds like a party," thought Monica. "I hope they won't mind my coming like this without an invitation." She stepped softly across the blue carpet, just brushing the piano, which responded with a soft note.

The voices in the dining room ceased and then someone said, "What was that?"

"I didn't hear anything. What makes you so jumpy?" replied another voice.

They were thin little voices and the diction was somewhat stilted — Monica would have said wooden if she had been asked to described it.

"I distinctly heard something," said the first voice. "Didn't you hear something, Colonel Charles?"

"It was *she*," said a third voice, also wooden but in a lower key and tinged with melancholy. "The moon has risen. She always comes with the moon."

"It wasn't *that*," said yet another voice, this one somewhat dry, not unlike the rustle of dry leaves. "I heard it and it was different. It was the noise of something about to happen."

"Things don't happen anymore," said the first voice.

Very cautiously, Monica made her way to the door of the dining room and stopped there on the threshold. The two Philadelphia dolls, in their crinolines, were seated on either side of the table, with the soldier at the head between them. The calico-skirted doll sat at the foot with her elbows on the table. The wax baby lay in the cradle beside her chair, rocking gently to and fro and staring at the ceiling.

"I thought that once," said Jerusha, "and I was wrong. Even after half a century something can happen. There's the niece who has arrived. I haven't seen a niece for more years than I care to recall and now here is one. So something has already happened."

"Very true," admitted Melinda and Belinda in unison, but the Colonel merely sighed.

"Come, come, Colonel Charles," said Jerusha — it was Jerusha who rustled like corn sheaves in the wind — "cast off dull care. We have the house. The garden will now no doubt return with the flowers, the fountain, the little nut tree. It was all very well to pine for a few years, but you've been at it for too long. Henrietta, may she rest in peace, is in the desert and there's no use in languishing."

"The desert is where I wish to go," replied the Colonel. "What is a garden without Henrietta? Fountains, peacocks, nut trees are not for me. Not even a silver tea-set can give me any satisfaction. Those things are for dolls who play croquet and drink tea. All the lovely lost things are in the desert. The jewels and the wedding dress — even the wedding itself — are in the desert with Henrietta. Rather the desert with her than a thousand peacocks."

"Splendidly put!" piped the baby. Monica jumped and found herself staring into the depths of his glassy violet eyes. "And now that the niece has come, perhaps she'll take you there to rescue Henrietta, and we can have the wedding after all."

"Oh, I do so wish I could," exclaimed Monica, forgetting that she had not been invited to dinner. "It would be wonderful to have the wedding. But I don't know where Henrietta is. And then there's the antique dealer."

"Bless my soul!" cried Melinda, shrill as a willow whistle, "the niece!"

"Dear me," said Belinda. "So it is. Come here, niece. Don't stand there gawking. It's bad manners. What's this about an antique dealer?"

"His name is Mr. Reels," said Monica. "That's all I know about him. Except that he's supposed to come and fetch you away tomorrow."

"Fetch us away!" exclaimed Belinda. "Fetch us away where?"

"To his shop, I suppose," said Monica. "I guess you're valuable and he can sell you for a lot of money."

"Oh, the wicked wicked boy!" lamented Melinda. "It

wasn't enough that he should ruin the wedding and lose Henrietta forever. Who would have thought that we should come to this!"

"When I think of the feasts we had," added Belinda, "the roast chicken, the cheese — And to think that I once considered marrying Sam Reels! But if he intends to sell us such a step is clearly impossible."

"The apples and the wine," wailed Jerusha.

"To say nothing of the bridesmaids' dresses and the revels we had in the garden," said Melinda. "This is as bad as the desert. It's worse. I shall fall prey to despair." And she flung herself into an attitude of despair.

"Oh, don't do that," said Monica. "Surely something can be done."

"Something *must* be done," said the baby. "We've been treasures for generations. We can't end our days as mere curiosities."

"We must fight for our existence," said the soldier. "This is clearly a time for heroism. I trust you can be heroic."

"I trust so, too," agreed Monica. "I've never tried it, but perhaps I'd better see about it now. But I haven't much time. What do you think we ought to do?"

"We can scarcely expect her to stand alone against an awful array of aunts and antique dealers," said the baby. "We must think of a plan." It rocked its cradle rapidly, obviously thinking hard. "You must resort to weapons of great subtlety. Pale faces and slammed doors, sighs, vapors, spleen. And if these fail, there are always inexplicable occurrences to fall back on. Strange coincidences, haunting recollections of the past, snatches of music, the scent of pressed flowers, fear of the unknown, apparitions barely glimpsed by moonlight, and even if necessary sudden claps of thunder and winds howling around corners and down chimneys. Long-lost treasures discovered. You must find Henrietta and the jeweled sword."

"Well, I'll be glad to try. But do you think it will do any good?"

"When you have discovered her," said the baby, "we shall have the wedding. There will be no further trouble with the antique dealer. He hates weddings. Always has — from childhood on."

"I shall help you," said the Colonel in his simple soldierly way. "I pledge myself to your service. Together we shall brave the desert and every other obstacle, and we shall find the bride — all in white, her eyes gleaming with surprise, and with her the sword, which I shall wear at my wedding."

"Why should she be surprised?" asked Monica.

"Henrietta is always surprised," said the Colonel. "It is one of her many charms."

"I expect it will be quite a surprise to Aunt Mimi too," said Monica. "Henrietta sounds marvelous. I don't wonder they were all upset when she got lost."

"Yes," said the Colonel. "She is marvelous. I think she is even more marvelous than we remember." As he spoke, the dining room seemed to grow brighter as the moonlight spilled into it. Looking toward the window, Monica could see the moth's shape filling the pane. She moved toward the moth, hearing the music box give forth its little tune. The moth was in the garden — Monica could see the curve of a pale wing over the fountain. She stepped through the French door with her hand outstretched to the moth and felt it brush against her hand. Then it was gone. She was standing beside the dolls' house in the gray light of early morning, the music still ringing faintly in her ears. Ban was standing beside her, his head cocked and his fur standing out in all directions. Monica looked down at the dolls, so innocently seated around the dining-room table waiting for the wedding, save for Melinda, who had fallen off her chair and was lying on the floor. What was she to do about them? Where was she to find the bride? What a crime to turn these lively creatures over to a hard-hearted antique dealer whose thoughts were on nothing but his profits.

People who bought houses, thought Monica, didn't usually acquire the inhabitants along with them. If Mr. Reels were to buy Wharton's Farm he wouldn't get Aunt Mimi, Winifred Price, Fred, and all the animals, too. So why should the dolls go with the dolls' house? The more she thought of it the better this argument sounded, but at the same time she wasn't sure how it would sound to anyone else. She looked down at the dolls for advice. It seemed to her that they looked at her beseechingly. She must save them. The wedding must take place; the house must not go. But how was all this to be managed? Standing there in the first dawn, she decided to begin by stealing the dolls. Stealing was not in Monica's line, but the more she looked at the dolls the more she felt that now was the time to do it.

She gathered up the lot, including the horse, and folded them in a breadth of black velvet that had been stored with them behind the gable, and crept across the attic, holding her breath all the way. As she reached the attic stairs she paused, seeing the darkness below her and feeling for the first stair with her foot. She must not risk falling down the steps with her arms full of this contraband. The darkness seemed bottomless and the idea of stepping into it momentarily terrifying. Nevertheless, she couldn't spend the rest of her life at the top of the stairs. Her foot was on the second stair when her heart skipped a beat. From the depths of the attic the music was tinkling, brisk and festive as though in celebration of something.

Monica turned and saw in the milky light that she had left the dolls' house doors wide open and that Ban was still standing in front of it, listening attentively. She returned to the house and shut it up. The music seemed to swell as the doors came together with an earsplitting creak. "How could anyone be sleeping through all this?" thought Monica, and she stood still for a moment, waiting for her aunt and Winifred Price to swarm up to the attic with pokers and possibly even firearms. Imprisoned in the house, the music fluttered faintly against the closed partitions but nobody came up the staircase.

Gathering her courage at last, Monica made her way down the stairs, hearing her own footfalls like thunder and feeling that she shook the house to its foundations with every step.

She reached her room with Ban following close behind her. The wardrobe bulged at her from its place opposite the bed and she opened it. Its hinges creaked noisily, and she gritted her teeth at them as she stowed the bundle of dolls as far back as possible. Then with chattering teeth she scrambled into bed.

Burglary was a new experience. Monica wondered what the penalties would be if she were caught. The worst her aunt would do, she hoped, would be to send the dolls back to the dolls' house, though some thoughts of dungeons and straw and bread and water crossed her mind. But then this was her first offense, so she might be let off with a warning. In any case it was too late for repentance. Day had nearly come, and the bedroom with its furniture was taking on its familiar daytime look.

There was a chilly daybreak breeze, and Ban was trying to creep under the covers for warmth. Monica pulled the sheet over her head, shut her eyes, and took a deep breath, determined to be found asleep in the morning.

Chapter 7

MONICA AWOKE QUITE LATE. Winifred Price had to call her twice to breakfast. The sun was high and the images of the night had already begun to fade from Monica's mind, making her wonder if the trip to the attic was nothing but a dream brought on by eating too large a dinner. She opened the door of the wardrobe and peeked under the pile of black velvet stowed at the back. The dolls were there. She shut the doors on them and went down to breakfast.

She found her aunt at the table, reading a letter.

"It's from your grandmother," said Mimi, fluttering the pages at Monica. "She wants me to give you the dolls' house. She should have mentioned it before. She sounds rather cross. Would it pacify you both if I were to leave you an enormous legacy instead?"

"What's a legacy?"

"Trust funds. Mansions. Incomes. That sort of thing. I shall leave you my pearls. You can wear them when you're eighteen."

"I'd rather have the dolls' house."

"And I shall give you a garden party."

"I don't like parties."

"You're impossible."

Monica ducked her head and began to eat cornflakes. Mimi changed the subject. "I hope you slept well," she said.

"Very well, thank you."

"Well, I didn't. I heard noises. I'm sure there are mice in the attic."

"Mice?" said Monica vaguely.

"You do know what mice are?" said Mimi sharply.

"Of course I do. But I didn't hear any mice."

"I'm astonished that they didn't wake you. Children always sleep like logs. They sounded like cowboys and Indians — when they didn't sound like piano movers. I scarcely closed an eye all night."

"I'm sorry about that," said Monica, staring at the sugar bowl. Could her aunt really have thought that mice had made that infernal racket for which she, of course, was responsible?

"Have you any plans for today?" asked Mimi, veering, to Monica's relief, from the noises in the attic.

"I hope I can go riding," said Monica.

"Suit yourself. Fred will go with you any time you ask him. Sam Reels will be here sometime to fetch the dolls' house. But you needn't pay any attention to him. He can manage by himself. I've a hospital board meeting in a few minutes. I shall probably be gone all morning. Winifred will fix your lunch."

"Thank you," said Monica. She was relieved to hear that her aunt would be so harmlessly occupied during the morning. She could have an undisturbed hour with the dolls' house before it was taken away. Perhaps she might even look for the bride. And if she found her, who could say what turn events might take?

She helped Winifred Price clear away the breakfast things and stayed to listen to an account of Winifred's daughter's graduation from high school. She excused herself after the presentation of diplomas and went upstairs to make her bed.

"A really well-brought-up child," said Winifred. "You don't see them like that nowadays."

"You'd better get some strawberries," said Mimi. "Children love strawberries. I remember never getting enough of them. And we should buy her some decent clothes. Children never have any clothes anymore."

Up in her room, Monica closed the door firmly behind her and then opened the wardrobe. She set the dolls in a neat row with their backs to the wall and began to consider their future. They couldn't remain in the wardrobe indefinitely. Her aunt would be bound to discover them. If they were returned to their house, then they would disappear with it, Monica would never see them again, and there would be no wedding even were the bride to be found, and this Monica could not bear to think of. And yet, how to frustrate the march of destiny as her aunt had devised it, seemed to be beyond her scope. But if she could save the dolls, they in turn might help her to a way of saving the house. Surely a niece and a handful of intelligent dolls should be a match for an aunt and an antique dealer.

She looked at the dolls severely. "Think of something clever," she said.

"Monica!" Mimi's voice floated up the stairs on a curl of cigarette smoke. "Fred will take you riding in ten minutes."

"You see," said Monica. "I have to make my bed and leave you here. There isn't much time. So you'd better think. They'll be taking your house to the antique shop before you can say Jack Robinson."

"Monica, did you hear me?"

"Coming," said Monica. And to the dolls, "Think."

She rode around the pasture three times, thinking hard herself, but to no purpose. Even the ride through the woods was no help. Green leaves clustered around her, and Nijjim waded through a little brook. Thrushes sang, and once she saw a scarlet tanager like a spot of blood against a patch of blue sky. She rode through stands of beech and through stands of pine. She tried to discuss the matter with Nijjim, but though he was a good listener, he contributed nothing. When she brought him back to the pasture after taking off his tack, he flung himself on his back and rolled and refused to give her his attention.

She strolled back to the house and found Winifred Price making sponge cake in the kitchen.

"Have you ever seen the dolls' house in the attic?" asked Monica.

"That funny old thing," said Winifred. "Yes, I've seen it."

"Aunt Mimi is giving it away to someone called Mr. Reels."

"That's right. It's time the attic was cleared out. I've told your aunt so a dozen times. That's what antique shops are for."

"Why would an old man like Mr. Reels want it?"

"There are more ways than one of parting fools from their money," said Winifred. "He'll sell it, of course. Sam Reels can sell anything. Provided there isn't any use in it. Pincushions marked out in pins saying 'baby.' Old spectacles. The hinges off barn doors. You wouldn't believe what he sells."

"I wish he'd sell the house to me," sighed Monica.

"You couldn't afford it. His prices are very high. Especially in the summer. That's when all the tourists come. If you only had some old gold now, you might get it in exchange."

"I haven't any old gold," said Monica.

"Too bad," said Winifred sympathetically.

"I wonder who will buy it," mused Monica.

"He'll sell it to a New York dealer. They come here and take his junk and fix it like new and sell it for even more than he does. Anyway, what would you want with an old dolls' house like that? You can buy a brand-new one in a shop any time. Why don't you ask your daddy to get you one?"

"It wouldn't be the same, and it wouldn't have the people in it."

"What people?"

"I mean the dolls."

"What do you know about dolls?" asked Winifred. "Have you been snooping up in the attic?"

"I wasn't snooping," said Monica.

"Well, how do you know about any dolls if you weren't snooping? You're big enough to know that you ought to let things alone that don't belong to you. Of course you were snooping."

"I only went up to see what the noise was about. The moth woke me up and I heard the music."

"Moth? Music? What music?"

"The music I heard in the night. Don't you ever hear it? It comes from the music box, French music, *Ah, vous dirai-je, Maman.*"

"Monica Mills, I don't know what you're talking about. There's no music in the attic."

"But I heard it. I heard it last night."

"This is an old house. It's full of noises. And there are mice in the attic. At least there were until the exterminator came. But I guess some of them got away so they're probably still up there. Your aunt should leave Ban up there for a night or two. He'd get rid of them fast enough."

"There aren't any mice up there. Only a moth."

"And the moth made so much noise — playing tunes and all — that you had to go after it. When were you in the attic, Monica?"

Monica blushed, furious at having given herself away so clumsily. "Last night," she said, "but only for a little while."

"You hadn't ought to have gone up at all without leave. Your aunt wouldn't like it. I hope you didn't touch anything."

"Well, I did. I touched the dolls. They were inside a little round hole at the top of the dolls' house."

"Well, I hope you left them *exactly* as you found them."

Monica said nothing.

"Well, did you?"

"No."

"What did you do with them?"

"I hid them."

"You *hid* them!"

"That's right. I hid them."

"And that's stealing. You unhide them right away. You take them back where you found them. Mr. Reels is coming for that dolls' house and he'll expect everything to be in it. You're a naughty girl, Monica. Go and get those dolls and don't let me catch you snooping around the attic again."

"You didn't catch me," said Monica. "I told you."

"It comes to the same thing. Run along and put the dolls back, and I won't mention it to your aunt. Make it quick now."

Casting an angry look over her shoulder at Winifred Price, Monica left the kitchen and started for the stairs. She climbed slowly, putting off the moment when she must open the wardrobe door and take the dolls back to their doomed mansion. And if the house was doomed, so were the dolls. They would be nothing but antiques with a DO NOT TOUCH sign in front of their house, their adventurous careers brought to a close.

They lay at the back of the wardrobe staring at the darkness, their painted eyes shining in the folds of the black velvet. They seemed to shudder slightly as Monica jerked open the wardrobe door. At the same moment, the doorbell pealed below.

"There he is," thought Monica. "Fate in the form of Mr. Reels."

"Monica," called Winifred Price, "have you got those dollies ready? Mr. Reels is here."

"They're right here," said Monica. She went to the head of the stairs and looked over the banister to see what fate looked like.

Mr. Reels was a shortish man, who, concealed as he was in layers of flesh, could have been almost any age between fifty and a hundred. He had round gray eyes behind thick spectacles and sparse sand-colored hair that stood up in spikes at the back of his head where he hadn't managed to comb it flat. His clothes were baggy and gray like his eyes. He wore earth shoes. They made him walk like a duck. He waddled through the hall and started up the stairs with an air of assurance, as though he knew his way about the house.

"Where's Fred?" he said to Winifred. "I need Fred. I can't carry that thing all by myself." He looked up at Monica, gazing down at him through the stairwell. "Who are you?"

"I'm Monica Mills."

"Oh. You look like a good strong girl. All girls are strong these days. You can give me a hand with the dolls' house."

"I don't think I can," said Monica, clutching at a straw. "It might be too heavy for me."

"Nonsense. A child could handle it."

"I'm a child and I think it's too big for a child."

"Anyone can see you're a child. A good strong one. I don't suppose," he said to Winifred Price, "that she has anything else she'd like to get rid of while I'm here?"

"She didn't mention anything," said Winifred. "Isn't the dolls' house enough for one day? You can't carry it as it is. How would you manage with anything else?"

"I was thinking of little things. Jewelry, snuff boxes. It's a shame to waste a trip. I can use anything she's got. I might just take a look around. You never can tell what might turn up."

"She didn't say nothing about anything," said Winifred. "Just the dolls' house. And you'll find it in the attic. So don't poke around. And *she's* got the dolls. Go get them, Monica."

Monica went back to the wardrobe, picked up the

pile of dolls, and returned to the hall with her armful. Mr. Reels was on his way to the attic. Monica followed him and deposited her collection, still wrapped up in the black velvet, in the parlor of the lovely house. She was near to tears. She would have wept had it not been for the presence of Mr. Reels. But he was of a type, she thought, to make tears useless. Monica thought he would not have known what they were.

"It's a shabby old thing," said Mr. Reels, screwing up his eyes. "It really hardly pays me to take it. It'll just clutter up the shop."

"Why do you take it then?" asked Monica. "Why not just leave it here?"

"Oh, I couldn't do that to Mrs. de Wardenour. It would break her heart."

"She thought it was your heart that would break if you didn't get it," said Monica. "She seemed to think you wanted it."

"Well, I don't — at least not much. I don't see why anyone would want it."

"Oh, I do. I mean I'm sure someone wants it."

"They do, do they? You don't happen to know what they offered for it?"

"No," said Monica sadly. She couldn't very well say that she hadn't offered anything.

"Well, I'm taking it," said Mr. Reels, "because I wouldn't want to see her get cheated. Her being a widow and all. Here's a box. Put all that furniture stuff in the box. I'll sort it out later."

Monica crouched down on the floor and began reluctantly to dismantle the house. She worked slowly, pausing over each object as she took it from the house. The things weighed heavily between her fingers, as though they did not willingly leave their places.

Mr. Reels swung round the attic, poking his nose into corners and behind trunks. "You never know what you'll find until you look," he said. He stopped and stared out the window and into the green confusion of the honeysuckle vine. He looked fixedly at the vine and even made a snatch at a tendril that waved over the dolls' house.

"What are you doing?" asked Monica, puzzled at this piece of pantomime.

"Nothing," said Mr. Reels. "Just don't want to overlook anything."

"I shouldn't think there'd be anything you want in the honeysuckle."

"You never can tell," said Mr. Reels. "Never. What are you dawdling over the house for? You act as though you'd never seen a set of dolls' house furniture before. Let me have a look at that tea-set. Hmn! Italian stuff." He thrust his hand into the house and withdrew it quickly. "Ouch!"

"What's the matter?" asked Monica.

"Something bit me." He was examining one finger. Like the rest of him, his fingers were pale gray. It came of pawing over antiques all day, Monica supposed.

"You must have put your hand on a wasp," said Monica.

"It's bleeding," said Mr. Reels. "It isn't a sting. It's a bite."

"That's ridiculous," said Monica. "Wasps don't bite. They haven't any teeth."

"Well, it must have been a mouse then."

Monica peered into the house. "There isn't any mouse here."

"Well something bit me. It's probably rabid. You can tell your aunt that if I die of rabies I shall sue her."

"Won't that be a little late?"

"Late for what?"

"I mean if you're already dead, what would be the use of suing?"

"I shall sue her before I die. Look in there carefully. Are you sure there's nothing there?"

"Nothing at all. Do you really want to take the house? Whatever it was that bit you might do it again."

"You put the rest of the things in the box. Whatever it was doesn't seem to want to bite you."

She gathered up the carpets, the pictures, the canary, and the King Charles spaniel and began to lay them softly in the box, one by one. "You must be very careful of the spaniel," she said. "He's made of china."

Mr. Reels cocked an eye at the spaniel, sitting in the palm of Monica's hand. "Gloucestershire," he said.

"Perhaps he bit you," said Monica. "Small dogs are apt to be fierce."

"Put it in the box," said Mr. Reels. "Collectors love those things. Myself, I never could abide dogs."

"Why don't you leave him here then?"

"I told you. Collectors love them."

"He really thinks it bit him," thought Monica, but she didn't say so aloud.

"I guess that's everything," she sighed. With all the resolution she could summon, she closed up the dolls' house. She had left the dolls in their heap on the parlor floor. She could not bear to touch them.

"You take one end and I'll take the other," said Mr. Reels. "We'll get it downstairs, and then you can come back for the box."

Monica lifted up her end of the house, Mr. Reels took his, and they started down the stairs, Monica going backward.

Mr. Reels was extremely clumsy, and he could not see

where he was going because the top gable of the house was higher than his head. And also, as Monica said later, the house had an earthquake. It began to dance. "Watch out!" screamed Monica. "It's flying." It flew out of Monica's hands, twirled twice, and struck Mr. Reels a stunning blow in the chest, knocking him flat so that he slid down the attic stairs and landed sitting on the hall carpet with Monica head over heels at the other end of the corridor and the house upside down between them. Ban rushed out of Monica's room and spat. Winifred Price and the Pekingese came tearing up from the kitchen. Ming began to bark in a high-pitched oriental way, displaying his aristocratic black tongue. Then all three stood pat, looking at the confusion as though it were a work of art.

Monica was the first to pick herself up, and she had the good manners to go to Mr. Reels's assistance.

"Are you hurt?" she asked.

"I should think I am. Seriously. Why don't you look where you're going?"

"I was looking the best way I could," said Monica, "but I was going backward."

"Anyone who would go downstairs backward needs their head examined," said Mr. Reels indignantly. "Look at those dolls. I thought you'd emptied the house."

Monica gathered up the dolls, who had all tumbled out in the fall. "Perhaps I'd better put them in the box with the furniture."

"Perhaps you'd better," agreed Mr. Reels. "I think I'll take the house the rest of the way myself. You might trip again since you don't seem to know how to look where you're putting your feet."

"It wasn't my fault," said Monica. "I never tripped. I was fine until you threw the house up in the air."

"*I* threw the house! I was holding it as carefully as eggs. The whole thing happened because you *would* go downstairs backward."

"That was the way you wanted it," said Monica angrily. "You've never even thanked me for helping you get it out of the attic. You might be there yet if it wasn't for me."

"Thanks to you I'm black and blue from head to foot. Go and get the box."

She picked up the dolls and took them up to the box without answering. She could hear Mr. Reels manhandling the house down the stairs to the entrance hall, and though he banged about like a June-bug he managed to make it to his pickup truck without any more accidents. She brought him the box and with a sad heart watched him drive away.

She went back to her bedroom and considered having a good cry but thought better of it. It would only end in red and swollen eyes. Her aunt would ask questions to which there could be only one answer, and the answer would annoy Aunt Mimi and serve no purpose. Biting her lip, swallowing hard, Monica stared at the wardrobe. The door was swinging on its hinges, and she went to close it. Something caught her eye in the farthest corner; it was almost as though it had moved. Monica put in a hand and drew out Colonel Charles, firmly mounted on the little horse. They had escaped.

Chapter 8

IT WAS SIMPLY MORE than Monica could do to chase after Mr. Reels with the information that the soldier and the horse had been left behind. She set the soldier astride the little piebald steed and then sat down in the overstuffed chair and looked at them. They had evaded the clutches of Mr. Reels for some very good reason. There was a meaning in this and Monica must find the meaning. She had stolen the dolls on purpose; now she had stolen the soldier and his mount by accident, and it seemed to her that accidents of this sort usually resulted in something if you didn't interfere with them. It was a matter of letting nature take its course. The course of nature seemed to show that Monica should keep these two. She considered the possible consequences.

What would her aunt say if she discovered that Monica stole things? Monica thought about a forestalling letter to her parents with overtones of homesickness but rejected the idea. Her father and mother would be in London by now, and it would be several days before a letter could reach them, and they could not be expected to fly back from England because of a toy soldier and a horse, however handsome. She might simply tie the two up in a red bandanna and run away, but where to? She would almost certainly be caught, and the goods would be restored to their rightful owner, Mr. Reels. The course of nature would be diverted and she would be punished. And the more she stared at the soldier, so gallantly a-horse, the more determined she became somehow to regain possession of the dolls' house. This she would never do by quitting the field. Monica squared her shoulders in a military manner and raised her hand to the officer in a small salute. No. She would not run away.

Monica wondered at the fairy godmother picture that her father had painted of his darling Aunt Mimi. Of course she had been younger when bestowing happiness on Henry, and perhaps she preferred boys to girls. People sometimes did. But she was less like a good fairy than a sharp, elderly child. Monica could easily imagine her playing with the dolls' house, browbeating its inhabitants and then neglecting them for some new fancy.

Winifred Price broke into these reflections by calling Monica to lunch.

"Seeing it's only lunchtime," she said, handing Monica a cheese sandwich, "you've done quite a lot for half a day. Stolen a pack of valuable dolls and nearly killed Sam Reels. What do you plan to do this afternoon?"

"I had nothing to do with his falling downstairs," said Monica. "It was all his fault."

"I know you," said Winifred. "You wished it on him."

"Nonsense," said Monica.

"Not that he didn't deserve it," pursued Winifred as though Monica hadn't spoken. "You won't be the first to have hexed him. Or the last. He's had problems of that kind all his life, or so they tell me."

"But I didn't hex him."

"Well, if you didn't, who did?"

"Nobody did, for all I know. He just fell downstairs. It was his earth shoes. They tripped him."

"He said he was bitten by something in the dolls' house."

"He just imagined it. There was nothing there to bite him."

"I saw the blood," said Winifred. "How do you account for that?"

"Well, I didn't bite him."

"Something did."

"Perhaps," said Monica, "he shouldn't have tried to take the dolls' house away. Perhaps it was trying to tell him something."

Winifred nodded. "You may have something there. His things have been trying to tell him something for years."

"Really? What have they been trying to say?"

"You'd understand if you saw his shop," said Winifred.

"Where does he keep his shop?" asked Monica.

"In Church Lane. Off Main Street down near the fish market. You go under the railroad bridge, and the house is just the other side. You can see the yacht basin just beyond it."

"Like a troll," said Monica. "He looks as though

he'd live under a bridge. I think I'll go and take a look at it."

"Why? Are you interested in antiques?"

"No. But I like shops. Thank you for the sandwich. Will you tell Aunt Mimi that I've gone to explore the village?"

"Since you're going to the village you can get me a can of coffee and a pineapple."

"All right."

"Come back at seven. If you're late I'll call the police."

"I can tell the time," said Monica. "I don't need the police."

She felt a little uneasy at this reference to the majesty of the law. She was plotting and her face probably showed it. Winifred Price was no doubt reading her like a book. She was surprised when the housekeeper made no effort to detain her but handed her a five-dollar bill and told her to spend the change on a treat.

Monica thanked Winifred enthusiastically, and then it flashed across her mind that since she was once more to set eyes on the dolls' house, the soldier should also have that opportunity. She ran upstairs again, took her canvas beach bag from the suitcase, dropped the soldier and the horse into it, and covered them with her bathing suit.

It was a hot afternoon. Monica walked through the village, past the Congregational church — white clapboard — past Passarelli's market where she bought the coffee and the pineapple, past the Laundromat, the Mobil station, the library, dark red stone with turrets, past the drugstore where she bought an ice-cream cone. She passed the post office, with its stars and stripes, an early colonial bank, a Gothic Episcopal church with ivy growing up its sides, a rectory to match, and a small nondescript building with a sign proclaiming that it was the Westmoreland Historical Association. Here the road dipped sharply under the railroad bridge and became Church Lane.

Mr. Reels's shop was an old red cottage in poor repair, sheathed in a greatly overgrown trumpet vine. It had once been the village sewing shop belonging to Mr. Reels's mother. Mr. Reels did not knit and had converted to antiques when his mother died at the age of ninety-four. There was a legend in the village that Mrs. Reels had died of laughing. All her life she had laughed at her brother, Harry Hobson, and when Harry died of being laughed at she had switched her laughter to her son and embittered his life. It was said that he resembled his uncle but was better educated. You had to be educated to go in for antiques. For a while he had sold spindle-backed chairs, patchwork quilts, and warming pans, but as antiques became ever more popular he sold iron stoves, chipped china, and things that people had won at fairs and had thrown out when they moved. Mr. Reels, as Winifred had said, would sell anything. He had a sign in his window saying SALE. People flocked in looking for picture frames, Queen Anne tables, Georgian silver, and Currier and Ives prints. They came away with cracked soup-tureens, old jazz records, lamp shades of colored glass representing grapevines, feather quilts moulting feathers, and other things that might come in handy. The shop was crowded from floor to ceiling with all these things and many more. Mr. Reels had tagged nearly everything at a hundred dollars and up but was ready to bargain. He had been known to reduce a price by as much as ninety dollars.

He had created alleys between the piles of merchandise barely wide enough for one person to pass through. Monica wondered as she stepped inside the shop what Mr. Reels would ever do if he sold the pipe organ, just visible under a superstructure of chairs, gate-legged tables, and church pews cut into sections, to say nothing of the rolltop desk huddled beneath two refrigerators and an Atwater Kent radio surmounted by a yellow vase full of ostrich feathers. Monica began a systematic search for the dolls' house under the glare of a stuffed moose head, among a variety of elderly photographs of fierce relatives in stiff collars and tinted portraits of bathing beauties of the nineteen twenties.

She came upon the dolls' house suddenly at the darkest end of the shop. Mr. Reels had placed it behind a small trunk over which Monica had to climb in order to gain access to her lost treasure. Its order and elegance were in sharp contrast to the debris that defined Mr. Reels. The box containing the furniture and the dolls was beside it.

Very quietly Monica began to rearrange the house. She spread the carpets and shook out the curtains. She set the sofa in the parlor and rehung the pictures on the walls. She placed the lamps on the tables and put the spaniel on the mat, stroking his ears and talking to him as she did so. She stood the grandfather clock at the foot of the stairs and placed the piano in its corner under the window overlooking the garden, which of course had traveled with the house. It was invisible now, but when the moon rose it would appear in its splendor of flowers and peacocks and fountains and the lawn where the dolls might frolic and dance to the tune of *Ah, vous dirai-je, Maman*.

She put the dolls in the parlor, including the baby, and

extracted the soldier and the horse from the beach bag so that they could all look at one another.

"Were you wanting something?"

Monica jumped and looked over her shoulder. Mr. Reels stood in the passage peering at her from behind his spectacles. The lenses were heavy and made his eyes seem much larger than they were. He goggled down at her. "Mustn't touch, you know. That house is worth a thousand dollars in case you're thinking of buying it."

Monica shook her head sadly. "No. I was just looking. I put the furniture back in." She glanced at him sideways. "I thought it would help."

"I don't know what you mean by help," said Mr. Reels sourly. "That house has already been a thousand dollars' worth of trouble."

"What do you mean by that?" asked Monica, puzzled.

"I thought I'd never get it here. First a flat tire. Then I hit a baker's truck. Ran right into the back of it. Destroyed every pie and cake in Westmoreland."

"You mean you had a flat tire and hit a baker's truck just between Aunt Mimi's house and here?"

He nodded. "My truck's at the shop now. I expect they can fix it. As soon as they get the whipped cream off it."

"I hope nobody was hurt," said Monica politely.

"It was the spirit of the thing," said Mr. Reels. "No. I wasn't hurt. It isn't what happened that I mind. It was the way it happened. Sheer malice."

"You mean the baker's truck backed into you on purpose?"

"Oh no. It was standing still."

"But then it was you that hit it."

"That's what everyone said. My truck deliberately ran out of juice. Just after I'd got your man, Fred, to put the tire back on. I was standing for twenty minutes in the broiling sun while he did it. I'd barely got started again. There's a short slope past your house. Down we went like a roller coaster. It was like some vampire had sucked the juice out of it."

"I'm terribly sorry," said Monica, trying not to laugh.

"And all on account of coming to fetch that dolls' house as a particular favor to your aunt."

"She'll be sorry too," said Monica.

"I should hope so," said Mr. Reels. His eye fell on Colonel Charles astride the horse. "What's that you've got there?"

"It's just a little soldier doll I found in the attic," said Monica, hoping he would not associate the two with the dolls' house.

Mr. Reels squinted at them. "I've seen them before," he said. "Seems like I met them somewhere. Something to do with a wedding."

"There was going to be a wedding," said Monica, "but the bride got lost."

"That's right," said Mr. Reels. "The bride. A real fancy doll. I didn't like her."

"Men don't usually like dolls," said Monica.

"That doll was a regular wildcat. She attacked my uncle Harry. And in my opinion, that soldier doll was in on it. And then, if you can believe it, she made off with a valuable piece of jewelry. I'd give a lot to know where that went. Oh, there's no doing nothing with those dolls. You can take that soldier away. I don't want him around. I don't like the way he looks."

"Perhaps I should take all the dolls if they worry you so," said Monica hopefully.

"No. You can leave the others. But that soldier has a mean expression. So does the horse. They're up to something."

"They look perfectly all right to me," said Monica.

"Don't trust looks," said Mr. Reels. "They can look as mild as milk, and then suddenly they're at you."

"They? Who?" asked Monica.

"Things," said Mr. Reels. "I have vast experience of things. Things come looking for you when you least expect it. You can't shake them off. I haven't seen that dolls' house man and boy these sixty years and now here it is. *Looking* at me. I'm going to show it who's boss. I'm going to sell it to the first comer. I shouldn't do too badly on it. There are plenty of folks who like that sort of thing. Those little wooden dolls, now. They're period pieces." He bent over and made a snatch at Belinda, who had fallen forward off the sofa. Melinda, straight upright, was simpering above the tea-things but Belinda looked riddles. "A genuine antique," said Mr. Reels. He stared into her face for a moment, stooped to put her back in the house, and then stood up, knocking against a table with two small chairs on top of it. A chiffonier with three legs was perched on top of them, and on top of the chiffonier were two hurricane lamps. The whole business came down on Mr. Reels.

Monica sprang to his assistance and began to pull the furniture off him and to brush the broken glass out of his hair.

"How they do come at you!" she exclaimed. "You really should be more careful."

"I'm careful enough," he said angrily. "If you hadn't left that cavalryman there none of this would have happened. He tripped me. Put him somewhere safe. Get him out of the way."

Monica put the soldier and the horse back in the beach bag, and the shop bell pealed loudly.

"Customers," said Mr. Reels and vanished down an alley. Monica heard a slight crash, indicating that something else had hit him, but evidently he was unhurt because the next moment she heard him greeting a customer. Monica came down the alley and into the main part of the shop for a better look at the kind of person who bought things from Mr. Reels.

The customer, a lady of stern aspect, heavy-set, red haired, and dressed in a fashionable pants suit, was asking for a warming pan.

"No warming pans today," said Mr. Reels. "Any day but this. I've sold them all. There's a great demand for them. But I can let you have a dolls' house."

"I don't want a dolls' house," said the lady, "but I'd like to look at some of your copper lustre if it's genuine."

"Copper lustre will cost you a thousand dollars," said Mr. Reels. "I can let you have the dolls' house for less. I can give you a fantastic bargain. You'd have something absolutely unique."

The lady appeared to be one of those who could not resist a fantastic bargain whether she wanted it or not.

"I'm not interested in dolls' houses," she said while following Mr. Reels to the back of the shop, nearly running over Monica in the process. "How much is it?"

Mr. Reels named a sum so gigantic that Monica thought she might faint.

The customer looked impressed. "That's a good deal more than I'd want to spend," she said.

Mr. Reels was looking sideways at the customer as though trying to guess her measurements.

"The house has a very interesting history," he said. "Belonged to one of our best families. They went to rack and ruin. Family tragedy —" he glared at Monica, who was on the verge of intervening. The lady had the look of a scientist being eaten by an octopus, fascinated in spite of her predicament.

"You don't say," she said.

"The eldest daughter ran away with the chauffeur. Son drank himself to death and went to jail. Old lady left all alone with her memories. Walks through the garden at night, wailing. Family jewels buried in the basement."

"I'll take it," said the customer breathlessly. "Will you accept a check?"

"I'll need some form of identification," said Mr. Reels, nervously clenching and unclenching his hands.

The lady busied herself with a checkbook and pen and with extracting a driver's license from her handbag. She proved to be a Mrs. Davis from New York and was staying for a few days at the Sunnybrook Inn, which stood on the edge of the town and boasted a nine-hole golf course and a swimming pool.

"I'll take it right out to your car," said Mr. Reels as she handed him the check.

"I thought I'd ask you to ship it to New York for me," said Mrs. Davis. "I'm not sure that Mr. Davis —"

"You wouldn't want to trust a thing like that to the express," said Mr. Reels. "No, you take it with you. You'll be happier that way."

"But Mr. Davis won't want to carry it in the car. What will he do with his golf clubs?"

"Believe me, he can put them in front. And once he sees this dolls' house he won't want it out of his sight. And think what you'll save on insurance."

"I suppose the family was very sorry to part with it,"

said Mrs. Davis, watching her check disappear into Mr. Reels's billfold.

"Heartbroke," answered Mr. Reels. "But think what the money will do for them. Dinner on the table. Clothes on their backs. You're doing them a good deed. Think of it that way."

Monica was so furious that she was actually plucking at Mrs. Davis's sleeve in her eagerness to contradict Mr. Reels, but before she could speak her piece Mr. Reels rounded on her.

"You!" he said. "You've been hanging around the shop all afternoon. What do you want here? Haven't you got a home to go to?" He turned to Mrs. Davis with a despairing gesture. "Kids nowadays! Nobody to look after them. Parents off on parties morning, noon, and night. Look at the poor little thing. Completely neglected."

"I'm not in the least neglected," exclaimed Monica. "I came to see the dolls' house, and I helped you to put it straight. How can you be so ungrateful?"

Mr. Reels winked broadly at Mrs. Davis, who now turned her attention to Monica. "Of course you did, dear," she said, "and I'm sure you were a great help. It was very nice of you." Mrs. Davis was one of those people who thought she understood children.

"I didn't mean it like that," said Monica. "And he hasn't hurt my feelings. I only meant that he's telling it all wrong. There's nothing the matter with my family."

"Nobody said there was," said Mr. Reels, "so why don't you go home to it?"

"You said that they neglected me," said Monica, "and that they needed —"

"Out you go," interposed Mr. Reels, and he swept

Monica out the front door as though she had been a stray cat. He slammed the door and she could see him through the window gesturing to Mrs. Davis, no doubt deploring the state of modern education. Monica rattled the doorknob, but he had slipped the bolt and she could not get in. While she watched him and tried to think her way through this stage of her problem, the church clocks struck seven, and rather than be taken up by the police, she trudged back to Wharton's Farm.

Chapter 9

ONICA HAD BARELY reached Wharton's Farm when she became conscious of a greenish glare crawling across the sky. As she stepped into the hall the house lit up momentarily in a flash of violet light and there was a crash of thunder. A prolonged and noisy storm followed. The Pekingese hid under the piano and panted. Ban walked up and down the porch and spat at the lightning. Monica played backgammon with her aunt in the parlor after dinner, but then the lights blew out so they both went to bed.

At the Sunnybrook Inn, Mr. and Mrs. Davis quarreled between rumbles and flashes over Mrs. Davis's new acquisition. Mr. Davis accused his wife of reckless extravagance, and she told him that he was stingy. The dolls' house occupied a corner of their suite and was intermittently illuminated by the streaks of lightning that tore across the sky. In spite of her husband's grumbling, Mrs. Davis could not regret her purchase.

"It looks very romantic with the storm playing over it," she said. "Like something in a novel."

"In novels there's usually a mad relative in the attic or a skeleton in the basement," said Mr. Davis, "and those things I don't need." He rolled over in his bed and pulled the covers over his eyes. Mrs. Davis considered reminding him of all the useless things he had bought over the years but then, realizing that he had fallen asleep, thought better of it and went to sleep herself.

In Church Lane, Mr. Reels had had an arduous day and had retired early. He slept right through the thunderstorm but he was troubled by dreams. He awoke when the moon appeared, gleaming through the scudding clouds and shining into his room. It was a round silver moon, and it jingled, thought Mr. Reels, like change in a pocket.

Mr. Reels sat up. "Drat that moon!" he said. "It's disturbing the things."

There was not only a moon but a wind. He could hear it in the trumpet vine outside the window.

"This is no climate for things," growled Mr. Reels. "They like it to be quieter. Perhaps I'd better make sure that the windows are shut."

He got out of bed, put on his dressing gown and his earth shoes, and started to shuffle down the stairs. Because he had forgotten to replace the bulb that had blown out two days ago, he could not switch on a light and was obliged to feel his way down the stairs, step by step. A breeze blew down his neck and grew stronger as he opened the door to his shop. The shop was very dark and full of the sounds that beset small, crowded places: the sighings and moanings of objects settling against one another, the small sound of dust sifting through shadows, the movement of moth and mouse and wood-worm. Mr. Reels paused on the threshold of his shop. One of the windows was open, swinging on its hinges, and the sound mingled oddly with the persistent tinkling of the moon. Mr. Reels went to secure the catch on the window, but before he could reach it a moth flew in, a huge pale moth with white spots on its wings. It hovered over Mr. Reels's head for an instant as though searching for something and then disappeared in the darkness at the other end of the shop.

"Get out of here," hissed Mr. Reels. "Get out of my shop. I know who you are, and I can tell you now that you won't find the rest of them here. Nor the house, either. You thought you'd catch me out, but I fooled you."

Perhaps the moth understood what he was saying. Perhaps it didn't. But it reappeared as suddenly as it had vanished, seeming to have grown larger. Its wings shook a pallid light across the darkness. Mr. Reels stood stock-still. He was lost in his own shop. Every familiar object was gone. Even the floor felt queer. He was not standing on a floor at all but on grass, damp grass that grew around his earth shoes. A garden was spread about him in all directions. Flowers spangled the lawn, and he heard water splashing in a fountain. He heard the cooing of doves, and a deer was gazing at him in cold curiosity from a thicket. Mr. Reels spun about in high indignation, looking for the malefactor who had caused a garden to invade his shop. He had some idea that there must be a conjuror somewhere with a top hat and rabbits springing from it, but all he could see was a baby — an elaborately dressed baby, wearing a crown and lying in a cradle under a hawthorne tree. A spaniel, whom Mr. Reels felt he had seen before, sat on a mat beside the cradle and kept the baby company.

"What are you doing in my shop?" asked Mr. Reels.

The baby looked at him with gleaming glass eyes. "As to that, what are you doing in my garden?"

"I don't know anything about a garden. I came downstairs to my shop to close a window. Now my shop's gone. And I don't like this place. I'd like to get out of here."

"A great many people want to get back to here," remarked the baby. "However, I suppose it takes all sorts. One of your kind just came. She's over there at the end of the lawn with the others."

Mr. Reels stared toward the end of the lawn, a sweep of green, and rising above it he glimpsed the pale wall, shining windows, and frosty gable of a huge house, which, like the spaniel, struck him as familiar. The house was so tall that the moon seemed to ride only inches above the roof. It was a beautiful house but it inspired fear. It was so vast. Mr. Reels's eye sought something smaller and rested finally on a gathering of people, four ladies, one in purple, one in yellow, one in calico — the color predominantly pink — and one standing a little apart whom he thought he recognized. He could have sworn it was Mrs. de Wardenour. He realized to his shame that he was about to confront her in his pajamas and would be at a distressing disadvantage.

"How the dickens did *she* get here?" he asked. "Why isn't she fast asleep in bed where she ought to be?"

"She's looking for something," said the baby. "But she won't find it. It comes of not looking in the right place."

"Well, I wish she'd go away. She looks as though she's coming this way. Go away, can't you? I'm not dressed."

She was walking toward him rapidly. He would have liked to have darted into the bushes, but he could not stir from the spot by the cradle. His feet felt as though they had taken root.

"What's she looking for?" he asked suspiciously.

"Any number of things," replied the baby. "Her spelling book. Her galoshes. Several husbands. The lost jewels."

"Well, where are they all?" asked Mr. Reels. "Never mind the galoshes and the husbands. Where are the jewels?"

"Odd," said the baby. "Are you looking for them, too?"

"I'm ready to buy them off her any time," said Mr. Reels. "I've told her so often. Old gold is what I'm in the market for. She palmed me off with the dolls' house. I took it off her hands as a favor —"

"You shouldn't have done that," said the baby.

"I don't know why not. I found a buyer for it right away."

"You shouldn't have done that either," said the baby. "It's not for sale."

"Do you mean to tell me —" began Mr. Reels, but before he could finish his sentence he was drowned out by a burst of music. Someone seized his hands, and he felt himself lifted off the turf and swung into a dance. He was dancing with the pink calico, but as he caught his breath to protest, he found his arm linked with that of the yellow crinoline. Then something jerked at his other arm, and he wallowed in the swirls of the purple crinoline, who clutched him and waved him triumphantly in the air. Mrs. de Wardenour was dancing, too. She seemed to be dancing with a moth, and she was scarcely visible behind a cloud of frosty wings.

"Come feast with us," chanted the dancers. "We shall give you roast chicken and apples and cheese and wine from our two decanters."

With a great effort Mr. Reels stopped dancing and stood squarely on the lawn in his earth shoes. "I can't eat that meal," he said. "It might disagree with me. It isn't real."

"I shouldn't worry about that," said the baby. "Perhaps you're the one who isn't real."

"If I'm not real," said Mr. Reels uneasily, "she's not real either." He pointed to Mimi de Wardenour. "And I'm not here in my pajamas looking like a fool, and she's not dancing fandangos around a garden that doesn't exist."

"Don't include me in this outrageous business," said Mimi sharply, catching sight of Mr. Reels. "I merely came here looking for a few things." She disappeared momentarily as the wings of the moth enveloped her, twirling her around a small fruit-laden tree. "It's absurd for you to pretend you're real, Sam," she continued as she reappeared. "What are you doing in this dream anyway? And look at you! I do think you might at least have worn a tie."

"Begging your pardon, Mrs. de Wardenour, but this dream was mine. And I think I'm entitled to wear what I please in my own dreams."

"There can be no question of whose dream this is," said Mimi. "And I came here on a perfectly straight-forward errand. I was looking for the sword, which you so carelessly lost."

"It wouldn't have got lost if you hadn't —" began Mr. Reels and then stopped in alarm. The moth was gazing at him with glittering eyes, smiling sweetly but staring through and through him. "*She* has it," he cried. "She knows where it is. She flew away with it and she's hidden it in my dream." He made a snatch at the moth and felt himself held back by fleshless wooden hands. They were huge. A giant gripped him. He saw eyes above him, blue eyes, black eyes, shining and staring. Somewhere in the distance he heard the neigh of a war-horse and the baying of hounds. He felt himself picked up and passed from hand to hand. "Give him to me. He's mine," cried a voice. The dolls were playing with him. He could hear that terrible baby shrieking with laughter over a surge of music. He struck out with his fists and felt himself sailing through the air. Then he hit the ground with a thud. Wings fanned his face, and the luna moth vanished into the darkness of Mr. Reels's shop. He stumbled backward into a leaning tower of tables. They came down in a heap. Two small sofas fell across the passage, straddling it and forming a bridge under which Mr. Reels cowered as the tables came down. He crawled under the sofas and finally reached the front of his shop, where he paused to take stock of the wreck-age and of himself. He had a few scratches but he found himself otherwise unharmed. But he was very angry and anxious to find something to blame for the fright he had sustained. The moon was no longer available. It had sailed past the window, leaving chaos in its wake, but Mr. Reels caught sight of the moth again, escaping through a broken windowpane. He grabbed the nearest weapon, which happened to be a parasol, and rushed to attack it, but by the time he reached the window the moth was gone. He fell upon several small pieces of furniture and beat them unmercifully.

"I'll sell you tomorrow," said Mr. Reels. "I'll sell the lot of you to the termite queen."

His things made no reply. The whole shop was irreproachably still. Mr. Reels went back to bed.

Mr. and Mrs. Davis rose with the sun, both of them complaining that they had spent a bad night. Mr. Davis claimed not to have closed an eye, and Mrs. Davis, recognizing the temper he was in, did not contradict him. The Davises looked haggard and unkempt in the early light but the dolls' house had a spruce, pleasant appearance, as though it had been refreshed by a shower of rain. Although the room was tightly sealed and air conditioned, Mrs. Davis thought she smelled damp earth and fresh grass. The dolls were bright-eyed and pink-cheeked — even a little flushed, Mrs. Davis thought, when she threw open the dolls' house to have a look at them. She must have jarred the house as she opened it, because she had a feeling that the dolls were not precisely as she had left them the night before. The baby was not in his cradle but was propped up on the parlor sofa, and Melinda appeared to have fallen off the piano bench and was lying on the parlor rug. Belinda and Jerusha were collapsed over the dining-room table among the food and the wine bottles, and the spaniel was in the kitchen. The furniture was also slightly disarranged — one small chair was upside down and the *Mona Lisa* hung askew on the library wall. Nearly every piece of furniture seemed indefinably misplaced. Mrs. Davis knelt down in front of the dolls' house and began to set it straight. The dolls wouldn't cooperate. They stuck out their arms and legs in all directions and fell over in awkward attitudes as though they had fainted. It didn't seem to matter how she pulled them about. They would neither sit nor stand. The baby lay stiff in its cradle, assuming a corpselike pose that was not pretty to see. Mrs. Davis came within an ace of chipping the spaniel. She rocked back on her heels and tried not to listen to Mr. Davis, who was in the bathroom with soap all over his face, shaving and nagging.

He couldn't think what had got into his wife, he said. "Look at the price of the thing." And where was it to be put? There was no place in the Davis apartment for a dolls' house. He didn't sweat it out all year in an office to buy dolls' houses. And a dolls' house that rocked and squeaked, from which strange music issued at dead of night, combined with the barking of dogs and bursts of hysterical laughter and sounds of people feasting and dancing, was not in his view a hedge against inflation.

Mrs. Davis said that it must have been the storm that had made him think he had heard all those noises, but she said it without spirit. She thought she had heard them too.

"And the music," continued Mr. Davis. "You can't tell me that lightning storms play music."

"It probably came from the bar," said Mrs. Davis hopefully.

"It wasn't that kind of music," said Mr. Davis. "It was creepy music. Long-haired music. Made you feel gloomy."

Mrs. Davis remarked that Mr. Davis had no appreciation of music.

"Well, I don't need a dolls' house to teach me fifty famous overtures. If I want to learn about them I'll buy eight-track tapes. Get rid of that dolls' house. I don't want it around. If you want the honest truth, it scares the daylights out of me."

It had scared the daylights out of Mrs. Davis, too, although she didn't care to admit it.

"I'll have to take it back to the dealer," she said. "He must exchange it — or give me back my money."

"He'll have to do just that," said Mr. Davis grimly.

Later that morning he put the dolls' house in the back of the station wagon and then went off to play a round of golf. Mrs. Davis made her way back to Mr. Reels's shop, driving slowly lest she jostle the house and offend its inhabitants. She didn't relish the idea of a confrontation, and it made her nervous to have the house at her back, breathing down her neck. It did nothing during the drive but merely sat smugly in the back of the wagon. There was, however, a confrontation with Mr. Reels.

He refused to consider the return of the house. He went from surly to truculent to downright menacing in the space of three sentences. Mrs. Davis pleaded and then threatened him with lawyers. He told her that he wasn't afraid of lawyers and stalked off into the little office where he kept his accounts, shutting the door behind him.

Mrs. Davis could not return to the inn with the dolls' house, at least she didn't think she could, so the only thing to do was to leave it on the steps of Mr. Reels's shop. With a good deal of difficulty she hauled it from the station wagon, hearing the furniture sliding about inside and half afraid that one of the dolls would pop out of a window and attack her. But she finally managed to place the house on Mr. Reels's front steps, overturning a pot of geraniums — valuable geraniums, Mr. Reels said later — as she did so. Then without further argument or explanation she drove away and spread the story all over town of how Mr. Reels had first cheated and then insulted her.

Monica learned of most of these details from Winifred Price.

"It just shows you," said Monica, "that it ought to belong to me."

"You don't mean to say that you still want that dolls' house!" said Winifred.

"Of course I want it."

"You're out of your mind. Look what it's done to Sam Reels."

"The difference between us is that I'm a little girl and he's an old man."

She took the first opportunity of assuring herself that the dolls' house was really there by paying a visit to Mr. Reels's shop. It was there all right. Flauntingly there. It was rooted to the spot on Mr. Reels's front steps and nothing seemed likely to alter its position. She took to calling on the dolls' house daily in order to reassure it and the dolls that she was not abandoning them to their fate, and her spirits rose so markedly that her aunt concluded that she had forgotten all about the dolls' house.

During the course of the next week Mr. Reels received two nasty letters from Mr. Davis's lawyers, and people in Westmoreland were beginning to talk. The proprietor of the inn advised Mr. Reels to get rid of the dolls' house as quickly as possible. He said it could be bad for business. Others disagreed. The owner of the gas station thought tourists would love it. They would drive for miles to see a haunted house.

Mr. Reels lurked in his shop, watching out for customers, and fretted. Several strange things occurred.

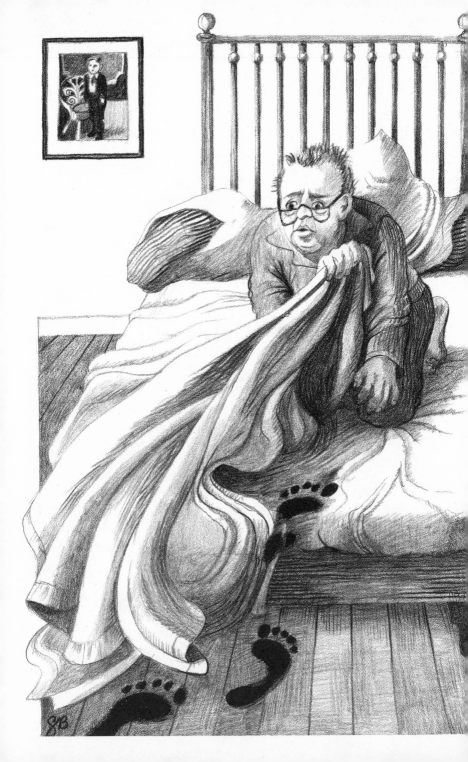

A barn roof fell in, injuring a tractor, and someone plundered Passarelli's Grocery of several hundred eggs. Mr. Reels was stung by a wasp and bought a gate-legged table that turned out to be a fake. His car battery ran down and a mouse in his shop scared a customer into a near heart attack. The owner of the drugstore started a rumor that the dolls' house not only was haunted but was a jinx as well. His wife said it wasn't so much the house as the dolls. They were the ones who were causing the trouble. The editor of the weekly town paper wrote an editorial on strange superstitions in New England.

And every day Monica sat beside the dolls' house, talked to the dolls, petted the spaniel, and even put fresh flowers in the vases for them while Mr. Reels glowered at her from the shop window.

"If it wasn't for all this loose talk that's flying around," he said to Monica, "I could get rid of that house in a minute. But people around here are scared to buy it now."

"But you've already sold it once," said Monica. "Why don't you just give it away if you don't want it?"

"Who should I give it to? They'd only bring it back like those Davises did."

"Not me," said Monica. "I wouldn't."

"It's valuable," said Mr. Reels. "You don't give valuable things to kids."

"But if nobody wants it — and you already got money from the Davises and you won't give it back — I should think it would hurt your conscience to keep it."

"Hurt my what?"

"Your conscience — you know — the still small voice —"

"Oh, that. Well, I'm a businessman. I can't afford to

hang around listening to still small voices like some people." And he stumped back into his shop.

That night Mr. Reels dreamed that an enormous moth was invading his bedroom and gulping down the blankets on his bed. He rose to defend them, and the moth paralyzed him with huge staring blue eyes, never ceasing to consume the bedding. He woke to find himself shivering under the sheet and the blankets in a heap on the floor. The window was open and the moon and the stars were giggling at him. He got up to close the window and knocked something off the shelf over the washstand, which stood in a small alcove near the window. The object broke, and Mr. Reels stepped in whatever it was that spilled out over the floor but was too agitated to do more than curse and scramble for his bed. As he discovered in the morning, he had spilled a bottle of ink. Giant blue footsteps stalked the floor from the window to the bed and the sheets looked as though some goblin had shared Mr. Reels's couch. He did not even wait to make himself a cup of coffee. He threw his coat on over his pajamas, emerged from his house, heaved the dolls' house into his pickup truck, and drove off with it toward Westmoreland woods.

Chapter 10

AT ABOUT THE SAME time that Mr. Reels was repairing to the woods, Monica was making ready to pay her daily visit to the dolls' house and cocking an eye at the weather, which looked threatening. The day was warm but overcast and it looked almost certain to rain.

The dolls' house would get wet, thought Monica. She was sure that Mr. Reels would never risk taking it into the shop again, so she considered that it was up to her to find a way to protect it. She went down to the stables where Fred was mucking out the stalls and asked him if he had such a thing as an old retired horse blanket.

As it happened he had. The blanket was frayed and dirty but it would last out a summer shower, and Monica, much pleased, set off with it for Mr. Reels's shop.

The blanket was quite an armful, and she was slower to reach the shop in Church Lane than usual. Mr. Reels had returned from his journey to the woods and was standing on his front steps scowling at the gathering clouds when she appeared with her blanket. She stopped and stared in dismay at the empty spot where the dolls' house had been.

"Where is it?" she exclaimed. "What have you done with it?"

"Where's what?" he said stupidly.

"The dolls' house. It's gone."

"That's right. Gone for good."

"You sold it again," said Monica despairingly.

"No, I didn't."

"Then, it's been stolen."

"No."

"You surely didn't take it inside," said Monica, sensing a thin ray of hope piercing the shadows of her dismay.

"Do you think I'm crazy?"

"No," she replied disconsolately. "I guess you're not crazy."

"I took it to the dump," said Mr. Reels. "To the town dump. That's where it belongs. The only crazy thing I did was to let it sit here on the doorstep worrying me. Worrying my shop. Worrying my things. And last night was the last straw. There were big blue footprints all over the bedroom floor. So I took it to the dump and that's the end of it. What are you doing with that blanket?"

"I was going to cover the house with it — so it wouldn't get wet. It's going to rain."

"Well, you're too late," said Mr. Reels, and he turned on his heel and went into his shop. "The landfill people will come and bury it," he said over his shoulder. "They'll bring the bulldozers."

Monica faced slowly round and started home. She was heartbroken and, for some reason that she had difficulty understanding, surprised. As she trudged up the lane toward Wharton's Farm she began to realize that up until now she had confidently assumed that somehow she would acquire the dolls' house. Someone — some unlikely person — would give it to her. People had given her things all her life, and she had thought that they always would. And now for the first time she was pretty sure that they had stopped this pleasant practice. It was beginning to look as though she would have to get the dolls' house for herself if she wanted it. But how was she to go about this? Even if she found her way to the dump — and she had no notion of where it was — how would she transport the dolls' house to a safe spot, one well fortified against its enemies — who were practically everyone. There was nobody to whom she could turn. Mr. Reels was out of the question. Aunt Mimi wouldn't help her. Aunt Mimi would say good riddance. Winifred Price and Fred Jackson would say that it was none of their business. With slow and mournful footsteps Monica lagged homeward. When she reached the farm she put the horse blanket back in the harness room. The barn was empty and quiet. The horses were grazing in the lea of the building, sticking close to home, as though aware of the coming storm. Fred had evidently gone off in the little truck in which he did his errands. Her aunt had gone out too, as Winifred Price informed her.

"We'll have some lunch here in the kitchen," said Winifred. "What's the matter with you? You look like you'd lost your last friend."

"Mr. Reels took the dolls' house to the dump," said Monica.

"Did he now?" said Winifred. "I thought it would come to that."

"Where is the dump?" asked Monica.

"It's in the woods. Just beyond Parson's Bog. It's about three miles. You can tell where it is because the sea gulls are always flying above it. But I wouldn't go there if I were you. It's a nasty place. And you needn't think you can drag the house back from there. Your aunt would never put up with it. She hates the thing."

"Mr. Reels says the men will come and bulldoze it."

"That's right. The dump's a landfill."

"Why should Aunt Mimi hate the house? Why shouldn't I have it if nobody else wants it? I think they're all absolutely hateful." And Monica burst into tears.

"Now, now," said Winifred, somewhat startled. "Don't say things like that. People like what they like and hate what they hate."

"That's right," said Monica, "and I like the dolls' house."

"Well, your aunt has her reasons. She's got bad memories about it. When you get to her age you're bound to have bad memories."

"She probably did something wicked, and the dolls' house makes her feel ashamed. Otherwise why should she hate it?"

"That's no way to talk about your aunt," said Winifred. "I don't see why you're so stuck on that old dolls' house. It's been sitting here for fifty years with nobody giving it a thought. Now you've got everyone stirred up about it. There wouldn't have been any fuss at all if it weren't for you. You're being awfully difficult."

"So are Aunt Mimi and Mr. Reels."

"They're grown-ups so they've a right to be."

"I don't see why they have any more right than I have," said Monica mulishly.

"Well, if I were you I'd stop being difficult around your aunt. She doesn't like it."

"Then I'll just have to stay in my room and be difficult there," said Monica.

"That's what they call sulking," said Winifred.

"And that's just what I'm going to do," said Monica as she started for the hallway. She was halfway up the stairs when there was a flash of lightning and an almost instantaneous roll of thunder. The front door seemed to blow open, and Mimi, with Ming at her heels, ran dripping into the hall, furious as a cat who has fallen into a goldfish bowl.

"Good heavens!" exclaimed Mimi. "Whoever brought this weather ought to be arrested. I'm drenched to the skin. Where's Monica? I hope she hasn't tried to go out riding."

"She's in her room," said Winifred. "Go into the parlor and light a fire. I'll bring you some lunch on a tray."

"I'm not in my room," said Monica. "I'm here."

Mimi looked up and said, "Well, come on down. You can have lunch in the parlor too."

"No," said Monica. "I can't. I'm going out."

"In all this rain!" said Mimi.

"It's because of the rain. I've got to fetch the dolls' house."

"Fetch the dolls' house!"

"Mr. Reels took it to the dump. It will get all wet and the men will come and bulldoze it."

"If it's at the dump," said Mimi, "there's absolutely nothing you can do about it. It's miles into the woods and there's a terrible storm. If Mr. Reels took it to the dump, that was where he wanted it. After all, it belongs to him."

"I want the dolls' house," said Monica. "Nobody else wants it. By a mysterious coincidence —" she said these words slowly because she liked their sound, "by a mysterious coincidence my grandmother wants me to have it too. It's as much hers as yours. You should have given it to me in the first place, but since you didn't, I'm going to find a way to have it. So there."

"Don't be impertinent. The house belonged to Mr. Reels before you ever got here."

"It doesn't want to belong to Mr. Reels. I should think that was plain enough."

"You mean *you* don't want it to belong to Mr. Reels. It would have gone quietly enough if it hadn't been for you. I refuse to have it here. It causes nothing but trouble. It's causing it now — with plenty of help from you."

"I do believe you're afraid of it. Imagine a grown-up afraid of a dolls' house! Two grown-ups."

"Nonsense," said Mimi.

"You're a dog-in-the-manger. You're both too old to play with the dolls' house but you won't let me play with it. Be careful it doesn't start to play with you. I'm going to rescue the house. That's what I came here to do."

"So it would seem," said Mimi. She gave Monica a long look of cold indignation. "You've made it all happen again. I should have been rid of it weeks ago if it hadn't been for you. You'd better go to your room. I'll discuss your behavior later. And don't let me see you again until I call you. I simply won't put up with this kind of thing."

Monica turned on her heel, ran up to her room, and slammed the bedroom door behind her, to show how difficult she could be if she really tried.

In the kitchen Winifred Price rattled pots and pans. Mimi put her head around the door and said, "What is that ghastly row?"

"Row!" said Winifred. "I thought it was you having a row. Still quarreling about that house?"

"Monica has a most unwholesome fixation on it," said Mimi. "She needs more company. I must think of something to take her mind off it. I should give her a party. It's too bad she isn't a bit older. I could give her a coming-out party."

"Girls don't have coming-out parties anymore," said Winifred.

"I know," said Mimi discontentedly. "One wonders how they get out at all."

"Oh, they get out all right," said Winifred. "But I don't think a party will work. It's the house she wants. She means to get it."

"It will have to work," said Mimi. "This dolls' house has us all by the ears. It's turned Monica into a sullen shrew with a touch of second sight. If I hear one more word about it, I shall have a nervous breakdown. I don't feel like lunch. Just bring me a cup of coffee." She went into the parlor accompanied by another roll of thunder, and Ming, who had been waiting for her there, dived under the piano.

"Coward," said Mimi. "Anyone would think you were made of china."

Up in her room, Monica waited for someone to come

up and scold her for slamming the door. She had slammed it so hard that the floor shook and the windows rattled, but after the room had settled down nobody appeared so she sat down cross-legged on the rug in the middle of the room and stared up at the window opposite, the one above the bed, where the honeysuckle vine encumbered the panes, thrusting its fronds at the sill and all but shutting out the daylight. There was not much daylight to shut out. She could see a few somber patches of sky through the lacework of leaves. The only light seemed to be gathered in the looking glass over the bureau. The little horse with the soldier doll astride him stood beside the pincushion. Both horse and soldier were looking toward the window as though they were expecting something. They were staring at the leaves and at the rain, which was coming not in drops but in rods, sluicing down the pane and pouring through the slit where the sash did not quite meet the sill. It was dripping down the expensive French wallpaper and onto the floor. Monica rose and went to shut the window. She found she couldn't close it. It was stuck, warped by the rain. She tried to loosen it by lifting it slightly and only succeeded in opening it wider. The drenched leaves of the honeysuckle vine tumbled across the sill and something fluttered among them.

"It's the moth," thought Monica. "It will be drowned in this downpour." She reached out her hand to rescue the moth, and her fingers closed around a handful of silk. She peered at what she held and encountered the sparkling eyes and charming smile of a small golden-haired doll.

She was more of an idol than a doll. She was dressed as a bride in white satin and pearls and her veil was

caught up in a loop by an elaborate gold stickpin with a head the shape of a sword hilt. The pin was stuck into the doll's silk and sawdust shoulder but since silk and sawdust were what she was made of she had suffered no damage. Indeed, she had been so well protected in her bower of leaves that she wasn't even very wet.

Leaving the rain to wreck the wallpaper, Monica took her discovery to the bureau, where the light from the looking glass showered down over the soldier and the horse, and examined her new-found treasure. Here certainly was the lost bride. She was immaculate and marvelously beautiful, smiling as unconcernedly as on the day she had vanished. Monica, feeling like the recipient of a miracle, set her on the horse behind the soldier and stood back in admiration. United at last, they sat together in the radiance of the storm to come to their long-delayed wedding. Gently, Monica removed the scarfpin from the wedding veil and attached it to the faded red ribbon that the soldier wore for a sash.

"He looks as though he were going to carry her off," thought Monica. "I suppose they'll go to look for their house."

A flash of lightning and a thunderclap startled her from her thoughts. Then she heard her name called sharply. Monica stepped into the hallway, reflecting that it hadn't taken her aunt very long to send for her — scarcely an hour had passed since she had been sent to her room.

"Are your windows closed?" shouted Mimi. "There seems to be some sort of flood."

"I'll close them," said Monica and returned to her room.

"I suppose she's been sulking in there, with the rain spoiling the walls, ever since I sent her upstairs," said

Mimi. "I know I shouldn't have lost my temper but she was incredibly rude."

"Well, most children are incredibly rude sometimes," said Winifred. "Weren't you ever incredibly rude?"

"If I was, I was punished for it. I wasn't allowed to play with the dolls' house."

"It's queer that you ever played with it at all, considering how you feel about it now."

"It's because of having played with it that I feel that way. The dolls' house punished me."

"Served you right, I expect," said Winifred. "If I were you, I'd make it up with Monica. Let bygones be bygones."

"Why should I?"

"Because she's a kid. You remember being a kid! Sure you do."

"No, I don't. I remember being me."

"Well, she's being her," said Winifred. "And funny things do happen. She might just be in the right."

"The right about what?"

"About the house, of course."

"Nonsense," said Mimi. "Stop talking about that house. It's gone. It went to the dump. They'll bulldoze it or burn it up or something." She started up the stairs. "I wager anything Monica hasn't closed her windows."

"No," agreed Winifred. "Her mind's not on windows."

Mimi threw open the door of Monica's room and was duly surprised to see that the windows had been closed, although a stain was visible below one of them where the water had spilled in from the vine. The room was almost dark, but as Mimi crossed the threshold a beam of lightning flashed in the looking glass and lit, as though they were on a stage, the soldier on the horse with Henrietta in all her bridal finery, as Mimi had last seen her more than half a century ago. Mimi screamed, scaring Monica nearly out of her wits. But then she recovered, caught up the bride, and held her out, flickering and fluttering in the half-light, toward Mimi.

"I found her," she said. "I found the bride and the jewel. It was slamming the door that did it. I knew I should do it somehow."

Mimi backed out of the room, shutting the door quickly behind her.

"Is there anything wrong?" called Winifred anxiously from the foot of the stairs. "I thought I heard a scream."

"I screamed," said Mimi crossly. "Who wouldn't? I've just seen a ghost." She ran down the hall to her bedroom and slammed the door behind her, giving the house its second big shake for that day.

Monica had supper by herself that evening. Winifred Price gave it to her in the dining room by candlelight so she could look at Henrietta propped up against a silver candlestick with a soft light falling on her satin and pearls.

Mimi kept to her room. "When people my age see ghosts," she said, "it's time to have dinner in bed."

So she went to bed, and Winifred Price brought her roast chicken and apple pie with cheese, and a glass of wine for her nerves.

"Your auntie's ill," said Winifred to Monica. "Seen a ghost."

"Oh," said Monica. "That was only Henrietta. Henrietta won't hurt her. Look at her. She wouldn't hurt a fly."

"So that's Henrietta," said Winifred. "Who would have thought it!"

"Who would have thought what?"

"Who would have thought a thing that size could throw a whole village into conniptions?" She bowed to Henrietta. "I'm certainly pleased to make your acquaintance. Goodness, what was that?"

"It's only the wind," said Monica, watching a slight gust make the candles sputter.

"How on earth did you find her after all these years?" said Winifred.

"I slammed the door."

"That was impertinent."

"Well, sometimes it's impertinent just to *be* a child. Anyway it was the right thing to do because it shook Henrietta out of the vine, and here she is. Now the only thing to do is to rescue the dolls' house."

"You've got that thing on the brain. Not that I don't think it was silly of them not to give it to you. But it's gone now, and you should start thinking of something else. I thought you were supposed to be crazy about horses."

"I *am* crazy about horses," said Monica with dignity.

"You're in luck. Taffy's going to foal any day now. Perhaps they'll let you have it when it comes."

"I should like that," said Monica, "but you're not taking my mind off the dolls' house. Horses!" Her mind shifted to the barn and the box stalls with bright eyes gleaming above the mangers. A horse. A horse was what she needed.

"Thank you," she said to Winifred, "for reminding me of the horses. But I think I'll go to bed now."

"At this hour!" said Winifred. "It's only eight o'clock."

"I know. But the storm was very exhausting. And what with Aunt Mimi's seeing a ghost and all —"

"I thought you said that Henrietta wasn't a ghost."

"I know I did. But you never can tell," said Monica.

"You certainly can't," said Winifred. "What's got into you? Going to bed at eight o'clock."

Chapter 11

HER ROOM WAS very dark. When she stepped into
it from the lighted corridor she had to feel her
way through it, brushing her hand across the mirror and
hearing the sigh of Henrietta's silks as she replaced her
on the horse. She sensed the presence of the soldier and
his bride but was unable to see them in the darkness.
Still, they were there, reflected in the dark mirror and
solid enough to cast their shadows when the moon
would rise.

"What shall I do?" whispered Monica. "The horses.
Nijjim. Little Star. How am I to find the desert?"

She went to the window and looked down on the
meadow. The rain had stopped. Taffy, the mare, had
been put in the barn, but Nijjim and Spectre stayed out

of doors in summer and were grazing quietly close to the barn. The sky was clearing and a star or two shone through the rents in the clouds scudding before the wind. It was going to be a fine windy night, followed by a bright day for the bulldozers. If Monica was to do anything, she must do it soon. But she had to wait for the household to settle down. She could hear Winifred Price's television clamoring from the kitchen, but Winifred would go to bed as soon as the criminals were captured and the commercials came on. Monica pulled a chair to the window, folded her arms on the sill, and put her head on her arms, giving herself up to thought.

It was silence that woke her. Suddenly in the stillness that had glided into the house while she had been thinking — or dreaming — at the window, Monica knew that the time had come. She could see from the window that Nijjim had moved into a stream of moonlight and was grazing peaceably, but even while she was looking at him she saw him lift his head and move sideways as though something had caught his eye. Something fluttered above his head and then drifted toward the window, drifted away from the pasture and around the house toward the honeysuckle vine where Henrietta had been imprisoned so long. For a moment it seemed to fill the whole pane with its wide wings, and then it rose and floated back toward the meadow and the little piebald horse. The moth was beckoning.

Monica did not stop to think or to pack necessary things. She skimmed out of her room and sped down the stairs, pausing, when she reached the hall, only long enough to decide that the kitchen door was her quickest and quietest way to the meadow.

"Nijjim! Star!"

He was pawing the grass at his feet, the mothlight

gleaming on his glossy black and white withers. Monica caught a tress of his mane and jumped onto his back. Before she was fairly settled, he had turned and was trotting off toward the woods beyond the orchard, the moth wavering and shining just ahead of him. When they came to the forest fence he jumped over it, landing lightly in the wood with Monica still on his back, slightly astonished but not at all afraid — everything that she was doing was so unexpected that she could not take the time to be afraid. The moth shed such a reassuring glow through the wood that she thought there was nothing to be afraid of. She felt well companioned — someone was guiding her.

Once in the wood, Nijjim launched into a smooth, rocking canter, moving through the woods to the music of the little frogs piping in the marshy patches. As they sped on their way, wild orchids lifted their heads from the swamp water, a fox paused on the track of a rabbit, and the rabbit leaped away into the shadows and to freedom. Two raccoons who were becoming engaged over a meal by the brook forgot their vows and turned their masks starward at the sound of Nijjim's hooves. A water moccasin hissed in admiration from the black pool where it lay, looking up through the water with prehistoric eyes. A trout on its journey upstream lay unstirring below the waterfall that hung motionless for a moment while Monica rode past on the little black and white horse. Through the woods she went past Parson's Bog to the desert beyond the wood, where all the lost things lay.

The wood ended abruptly where the world began — the worst of the world. Monica saw patched hoardings and thickets of rusty metal. Broken glass, torn curtains, silent clocks, wasted playthings, cheap and nasty things, once beautiful things, now through no fault of their own grown hideous, littered the hard-packed ground. The desert stretched as far as Monica could see, a cluttered acre where small sullen fires sputtered and smoldered among the rubbish — hungry little fires, always famished, always feeding, but never getting enough to flare into one big blaze and make an end to this desolation. This was the desert. This was where all the castaways of people's lives went. This was where every unwanted thing lay rotting and spoiling, past all rescue, and this was where the moth and the horse had brought Monica.

And then she saw the house. She hardly knew how it had happened, but Nijjim was standing in front of it, whinnying as though suggesting that she dismount. She slid from his back, ran to the house, and threw open the doors.

The house was in perfect order, as though made ready for a festival. For a moment Monica stood gazing up at the lofty ceiling, so high that she thought she saw a star in it. She touched the cold columns on either side of the fireplace. She let her fingers fall lightly on the ornaments and across the curtains. She caught a glimpse of her own enraptured face in the shining surfaces of the tables and the mirrors. Everything could be touched and when touched proved to be exactly what it seemed to be. The marble was real, the silk rustled under her hand. She could smell wet earth from the garden, and the light that streamed through the windows was warm. The house and the garden were as real as Monica's love of them.

Then a sound fell on her ear. *Ping — ping*. And the music rose in a wave of sound, the triumphal march of the lost things made real again. The house shook with sound and thronged with presences.

Monica stepped to the window and saw by the light of the now westering moon the garden celebrating the return of the bride, Henrietta, from her long exile. She was dancing around the fountain with the soldier. Melinda and Belinda danced through the orchard, and Jerusha with the baby in her arms danced around the little nut tree with the golden pear. The horse danced, lifting his feet high, like a circus horse, and the china spaniel gamboled among them all.

Without waiting for an invitation, Monica ran into the garden and it was Henrietta who held out her arms and cried: "Here you are at last! I thought you would never come."

"I came as quickly as I could," replied Monica, "but it was a long journey."

"A long journey indeed," said Henrietta, "fifty years and more. But now you are here. Our revels can begin. Let all the lost things assemble, for Monica Mills has found them."

Then from the desert the lost things came, by twos and threes, and in clusters. They came in shining shapes of jewels and metal, and they came softly as satin and velvet. There were creatures carved of wood and ivory, and of glowing stone. There were lost stories, forgotten tunes, scissors and school books, galoshes and coral necklaces, sunken galleons, people's wits, the fish that got away, and the snows of yesteryear, all in a glitter in the garden, come to celebrate the slamming of a door and the shaking of a honeysuckle vine.

Even the wild things came: the lost wilderness and the creatures that had vanished with it. The fox and the rabbit came, and the two raccoons who were celebrating their engagement, two owls, and the bat who had courted Henrietta. A weaving spider drifted in at the end of a shimmering thread, and a drowsy beetle and a spotted snake with double tongue.

Jerusha and Melinda and Belinda spread a feast for this distinguished company, roast chicken, cheese, apples, and wine from the two decanters. And the feast was followed by light entertainment. Henrietta spun a stack of straw into golden mittens. Jerusha cast a flower into a hundred years' sleep, and the baby caused a century to flash by in the twinkling of a star.

"And now," said the baby, when the applause that followed these interesting performances had subsided, "it is time to call the wedding to order. Now, by the authority invested in me as Crown Prince of Broceliande and the surrounding territories, I declare that the wedding between the gallant and irreproachable guardsman, otherwise known as Colonel Charles, and Henrietta, spinster, late of —"

"Oh, no you don't," cried a harsh voice at Monica's elbow. She turned to face a large sea gull who must have blundered in from the landfill with the other mislaid objects and now shouldered his way up to the bride and groom and stood ruffling his wings and shifting from one foot to another. It was impossible not to recognize beneath the feathers the form and substance of Mr. Reels.

"Oh, no you don't. Not until I get what I came for. There it is, stuck in his sash where it was in the first place. Old gold. Old gold. I always knew I'd find it at last. Finders keepers."

"Oh, no *you* don't," cried Monica. "You've spoiled the wedding once. You shan't spoil it again. Go away."

"Weddings. Weddings. Weddings are stupid. I don't want to play weddings. I'm a business bird and I don't hold with all this romancing. Here! What's all this? What do you think you're doing?" He addressed himself to a firefly who had flung itself at him violently, its lamp fairly sizzling.

"Lost, lost, lost," crackled the firefly. "You lost the bride and the jewel. They're in the desert, where all the lost things go, and good riddance. They're all ghosts. Leave them to the bulldozers."

"Wrecked my shop," grumbled the sea gull. "Flattened my tires, ran me into a pastry truck. Set the customers against me. Give me the old gold and I'll go away and be good."

"Chittered and squeaked all night," complained the firefly. "Wind and rain and footsteps in the night. Mocked and made off with things."

"There, there," said Henrietta soothingly to Monica. "They lost their childhoods. They must be here somewhere. Everything else is. If they find them, they will stop disturbing us. Somewhere here there are two lost childhoods." Monica looked around among the medley of lost things and suddenly she saw them — standing on the far side of the fountain, two little ghosts, a boy and a girl, one wearing brown knickers and a cross expression, the other a middy suit and an equally cross expression. They were squabbling.

"Oh, do stop it," exclaimed Monica. "We're going to have the wedding and you're interfering with it." She started to run toward the children but was distracted by the sea gull, who stretched out his neck with a squawk and tried to pull the sword out of Colonel Charles's sash. The firefly made a sound like frying bacon, and simultaneously a huge moth swooped down and engulfed the sea gull and the firefly in a cloud of white wings.

They all rose in the air together and slid into the sunlight that reached across the eastern sky and gathered them into the morning.

It was morning everywhere. A cock crowed. The house, shrunk to its daylight size, stood desolate in the landfill. The company was fled, the banquet had vanished, the music was hushed, and only the luna moth hung spread-eagled across the window of the gable. The dolls' house stood in the dismal wasteland where Mr. Reels had left it.

It was a scene of hopelessness. Nijjim was pawing discontentedly at the barren turf, indicating that he could not stay here all day with nothing to eat. Yet Monica could not abandon the dolls' house. Then, just as she had made up her mind to remain forever at the landfill, she was distracted and appalled by a fierce grinding of gears and the sight of a yellow monster moving slowly but purposefully across the dusty acre toward her and the dolls' house.

The monster was manned by a driver and a companion who was the first to catch sight of Monica semaphoring and shouting from the pile of refuse where the dolls' house stood.

The machine came to a stop, and Monica ran across to it. "You're the very people I came here to prevent. I'm so glad you've come. You mustn't bulldoze the dolls' house, but you're just the thing to take it home for me."

The driver and his assistant both climbed down from the bulldozer and peered at Monica. They seemed not to understand what she was saying nor did they look pleased to see her.

"You see," said Monica, trying to speak slowly in order to get her point across, "now that you've come, you can bring it home. I thought perhaps Nijjim could carry the house on his back but I've nothing to tie it on with. I didn't even bring his saddle last night. I rode bareback. And I can't carry the house by myself. It's three miles to where I live through the woods. But it would be nothing for you to take it. And please, won't you do it right away because they don't know I'm out, and if they wake up and find I'm gone they'll be furious, and perhaps they'll take the house away again — for a punishment, you know. And so I must get home so we can have the wedding. It's been put off for fifty years and it would be a shame to wait any longer."

The driver of the bulldozer could think of nothing better to say than, "Fifty years."

"Yes, fifty years," said Monica impatiently. "That's long enough."

"They ought to have made up their minds by now," agreed the man. "What was it you said you wanted me to do?"

"I want you not to bulldoze the dolls' house —"

"I won't," said the man.

"And I want you to take it home — on your bulldozer. It's only to Wharton's Farm and it's only three miles. It won't take you long and I — I — I'll ask Winifred Price to give you some coffee and cakes — or whatever else you'd like — only please take the dolls' house home. You don't even have to take me. I'll ride Nijjim — slowly in front of you so you won't get lost."

"I know the way," said the man. "But I don't see what you're doing here at this time of the morning when someone's getting married at your house."

"Oh, they'll wait for me," said Monica. "In fact, they can't get married without me."

The second man spoke up. "We'd better do like she

says," he said. "We'd better get her home and let some-one else take the responsibility."

"I guess you're right," said the driver. "I wouldn't want to get mixed up in anything."

"Oh thank you, thank you," said Monica. "Truly, you'll never regret this. Never."

"I don't aim to," said the driver shortly.

"And now," said Monica happily, almost to herself, "we can get on with the wedding."

"I wouldn't want to hold up a wedding any longer," said the driver, "not after fifty years."

He walked over to the dolls' house and heaved it up and with the assistance of his companion established it firmly in the bulldozer. Monica scrambled onto Nijjim's back and the small cavalcade then set off across the land-fill and turned onto the dirt road that led in turn to the highway. Thus an hour later, with all deliberate speed, the bulldozer drove up the driveway of Wharton's Farm and awakened Mimi with its noise.

She jumped from her bed and ran to the window just in time to see the two men unload the dolls' house, place it carefully on the steps of the verandah, and then drive off, a yellow dinosaur, lumbering on its way to some prehistoric feeding ground.

Resignedly Mimi lit a cigarette. There was no point in making a fuss.

Chapter 12

Y OU CAN'T FIGHT MAGIC and modern machinery," said Mimi. "One or the other, perhaps, but not both. So I suppose the wedding is on."

"Oh, yes," said Monica. "It's on. It's this afternoon. You must come."

"I'll come," said Mimi.

"Good," said Monica. "And Winifred too. I'd thought of asking Mr. Reels but I don't suppose he'd care for it."

"I don't suppose he would," said Mimi.

So Monica held the wedding with pomp, with triumph, and with reveling. Winifred Price made a cake and Mimi donated a bottle of vintage ginger ale. Colonel Charles had never looked handsomer nor Henrietta more lovely. And when the last notes of the music box had died away, Mimi formally presented Monica with the dolls' house. She said that Monica had earned the house. Mimi had always regretted the loss of the scarf-pin and Monica had found it after all this time. In a burst of generosity, she bestowed the trinket on Monica, who promptly restored it to Colonel Charles, its rightful owner. It came in handy in the various adventures in which he was engaged during the rest of summer.

Mimi made a present to Mr. Reels of the butter dish that she had bought at the auction on the day of Monica's arrival at Wharton's Farm. It was old gold, or at least silver gilt, and made a good consolation prize.

Later that summer, rather to Monica's annoyance, Mimi gave a party and invited some nice young people for Monica to meet. They came amid a gaggle of grown-ups, including Mr. Reels, and Monica invited them up to her room to see the dolls' house. She invited Mr. Reels too, but he wouldn't come.

"I've seen enough of that thing to last me a lifetime," he said. "If I had my way it wouldn't be here now. You'll be taking it with you when you leave, I hope."

"Of course," said Monica.

"I'm not superstitious, mind you," said Mr. Reels, "and I don't hold with dreams and astrology and all that stuff, but I wouldn't travel with it. My advice would be to send it by express and then go the long way round yourself."

"I don't think it would be dangerous for me to travel with it," said Monica. "I understand its ways."

"Suit yourself," said Mr. Reels. "But I'll be glad when it leaves town." He drifted across to the refreshment table, leaving Monica with one of the nice young people, "a girl of your own age," named Anne Forester. She was an attractive girl, Monica thought, looking slightly like Henrietta, or would in later life when the bands came off her teeth.

She invited Anne upstairs once more, and they played with the dolls' house all afternoon. They celebrated the wedding again especially for Anne's benefit and served quite a bit of the party food. "The beauty of it is," said Monica, "that I can have as many weddings as I want."

They left their ceremony reluctantly when Mimi called them downstairs to say that there was a surprise for them.

"Go to the stable," she said. "Go softly."

Taffy, the mare, was in the stable. Fred was with her. She had had a busy day, he said. She had dropped her foal, a piebald colt. He stood in the stall beside his mother, perfect in every particular, like some marvelous toy with a soul.

"If he only had wheels," said Anne, "he'd be just like your little horse upstairs."

The girls lingered long in the barn watching the mare and her foal until they became invisible in the shadows. Then Fred turned the children out of the barn, and they walked slowly back to the house. It was nearly dark, and only a few of the party guests remained talking in the twilight. Winifred Price switched on the porch lights, attracting a cluster of moths.

"What's that noise?" asked Anne suddenly.

"What noise?"

"There it is again. Someone's playing music."

Faintly across the dusk drifted the little tune, *"Ah, vous dirai-je, Maman."*

"It's just the dolls' house," said Monica. "I forgot to tell you. It's haunted. Sometimes I think my aunt haunts it." She burst into giggles.

Anne giggled, too. "Do you really? I wish I had a haunted dolls' house." They stood very still under the window through which the music chimed. In the darkness, Nijjim cantered away to the far end of the pasture, leaving a surge of silence in his wake.